WHEN DARKNESS FALLS
Grace Gray Sample

Fearing the wrath of her tyrannical husband, Anthony, Elaine Bradford bundles up their three-year-old daughter, Amanda, and leaves him. Unfortunately, Aaron, Anthony's son from a previous relationship, catches them in the act and begs to go with them. Now fearing that Anthony will have her charged with kidnapping, Elaine runs to the only person she can trust—her friend Emma.

Emma is the assistant to Laurie Lee Randall, the founder and CEO of the Laurie Lee cosmetic empire, who has agreed to let Elaine hide out at her New England farm until she can divorce Anthony and get her life back on track.

However, Anthony is a powerful man whose contacts are everywhere, and Elaine is easy to track down. When Elaine realizes what Anthony is after, she tries everything in her power to keep her daughter safe and regain her freedom. But all that she trusts is tested, and soon she discovers that everything she believes is not at all what it appears.

Other books by Grace Gray Sample:

While She Was Sleeping

WHEN DARKNESS FALLS

•

Grace Gray Sample

AVALON BOOKS
NEW YORK

PRINTED IN THE UNITED STATES OF AMERICA
ON ACID-FREE PAPER
BY HADDON CRAFTSMEN, BLOOMSBURG, PENNSYLVANIA

For all of my children, Judy, Wayne Jr. (Lee), Gary, Joyce, David and Guy, whose loving help and concern has always been and will always be appreciated.

Chapter One

Something, some noise inside the house or outside had awakened her. She lay very still in the lumpy bed she had slept in for most of her eleven years and listened, hardly breathing. All she could hear was the pounding of her heart.

The normal sounds she liked to hear were hushed, as if the twittering birds and the restless animals of the Ozark forest waited, too, for the sound to be repeated.

Low and muffled, it came again, then died away, blending into the moan of the night wind before she could be absolutely certain that she had heard anything.

The sound of heavy footsteps thudded across the wood floor of the next room, pausing outside her door. Was her father just now going to bed? Or had he been disturbed from his drunken slumber by the same noise she heard?

The door knob rattled. She turned over in bed to face that direction, her eyes straining to see through the darkness of the dingy room. The heavy wooden door creaked open, first a crack, then all the way on protesting hinges.

Her father stumbled toward her. He swung the lantern he was carrying up above her bed, letting the glow fall on her face.

"Awake, are ya?"

1

"What's the matter?" She sat straight up, holding the ragged quilt close to her chin.

"Get up," he barked, his gaze slid across her face, then he turned abruptly and banged the lantern down on an old dresser by the door. As he backed out of the room he added even more sharply, "Get dressed."

She got out of bed and pulled her thin cotton dress on over her head. Taking the lantern by the bail, she carried it with her into the kitchen, crossing the cold, gritty floor on bare feet.

"What's the matter?" she asked him again as she joined him by the open outer door. Wordlessly, he reached a hand for the lantern, and stepped out into the dark night. The moon cast shadows all around as she followed him across the yard. The stars shone down, distant and white.

"It's your brother," he said.

Though not knowing what was wrong, his words and his tone were ominous sounding. She shivered, but not from the cold. The wind that sighed through the ancient pine trees carried a mournful, sorrowful wail that chilled her very being.

"He's gone," were her father's next words. There was no emotion in his voice, but they lashed at her cruelly. Buddy was two years younger than she—where could he have gone to in the dark of the night?

"Gone? Gone where?" she cried out, pressing closer, trying to see up into his face.

"He fell down the well. You've got to help me get him out."

Her mind reeled. What could he have been doing out here at this time of night? How could he have fallen over the rock-lined well? Even in the daytime they never played there. Drawing water up past the rough rocks was a daily chore, their only means of water for cooking and bathing.

She hurried closer. The board top was propped up against the stone wall that protruded out of the ground. Her father swung the lantern down into the hole, bending over to peer down the shaft that yawned open, black and forbidding.

She dropped on bare knees down at the side to peek over the edge. A damp, moldy smell wafted upward. A loose rock rattled and fell, hitting the water seconds later with a faraway splash. She screamed her brother's name, calling out, "Buddy, Buddy," over and over again, her voice high and shrill, echoing like a sob through the night.

"Take the lantern," her father ordered. "See if you can see him down there. I'll put the rope down." He handed her the lantern and got a rope that was coiled under a nearby tree. He fastened one end around the trunk and let the other end slither past her down into the hole.

Though she held the lantern as far down as she dared, the flickering yellow flame did little to penetrate the darkness below.

A sound from behind caused her to whirl around. Her back pressed against the low curb as she thrust the lantern upward.

Her father stood above her, weaving drunkenly from side to side, a massive rock held in his hands high over his head. The light reflected strangely in his eyes.

He lunged at her with the stone. On her feet now, she lurched backward, hanging for one terrifying minute onto the rough, cold stones before feeling herself slipping and falling downward. A rock rolled. She heard a splash below.

"Father," she screamed, her fingers digging into the rocks, clutching and scraping, tearing her nails as she tried to cling to the slick wet surface.

There was no answer. She groped higher. Her bare toes dug desperately into a crevice. Her arms ached from the weight of her body. The opening above her appeared small, and far away.

"Please, God," she begged silently.

So intent was her struggle that she forgot the rope that dangled beside her, within reach.

Chapter Two

Thirty-Five Years Later

Tense, but determined to put distance between her and what she left behind in Chicago, Elaine Bradford, a slim, trim young woman of twenty-nine, accelerated the engine as she sped on Interstate 80 across northern Illinois. Leaving Illinois behind at Rock Island, she drove into Iowa at Davenport. She drove fast, but carefully, keeping watch in the rearview mirror for a car she did not want to see.

Weary from driving and from the fear that she was being followed, she'd stopped only those times when three-year-old Amanda demanded to "go potty now."

A sense of relief flooded over her as the hours passed and she could finally turn south with no sign of the familiar long black car that Martin Sills drove.

Amanda was nodding off in her car seat. Elaine realized the child must be hungry for something other than the crackers and peanut butter and boxes of orange juice she'd given her and Aaron, but she hadn't stopped in spite of Amanda's fussing. Aaron, ten, had been unbelievably good. Most of the time he'd been interested in the timber and the rolling hills, and then the flat acres where huge machines tripped out big round bales of hay that gave him something different to look at, to ask questions about.

"Will the farm where we're going be like that?" he wondered, pointing out an especially attractive farm setting complete with red barn, a two-story farm house with a picket fence across the yard, and animals roaming in the pasture behind woven wire.

"I've never been to the place we're going," she answered. "Emma Madison, a good friend of mine, lives there. When I called her, she told me to come."

"She has a farm?" Aaron was duly impressed.

"No-o-o," Elaine answered slowly. "She works there. She's lived there ever since she left Chicago. I used to work with her. She's a very nice person." After a moment she added, "I don't think it's an ordinary farm. Emma told me one time that they raise pheasant."

Elaine drove on, lost in thought, and glad to see that Aaron had curled up against his half-sister's car seat and was dropping off to sleep, too.

What would Emma say about Aaron being with her, especially when she learned how far Elaine had gone in carrying out that decision to bring him with her and Amanda?

Surely Anthony knew by now that she was gone and had taken both of the children. Sometimes Anthony would be away all day, not returning home until late at night after she and Amanda had gone to bed. And if he was home, he usually shut himself up in his den to carry on with his business.

Their absence might not be noticed at first. Still, it would be impossible for one of the maids, or for Aaron's grandmother not to have missed him by now, which would lead to the discovery that she and Amanda were gone, too.

She resisted the impulse to turn on the radio. If Anthony had involved the police in their disappearance a newscaster might announce it, Aaron might hear that they were looking for them and realize that his begging to go with her had not been the right thing to do.

She knew she had no legal right to take her stepson. During their four years of marriage, Anthony never gave her permission to regard his son as part of *their* household.

When they were first married she had suggested that Aaron be allowed to live with them only to be told in precise and cold words that Aaron was none of her business.

"I just thought . . ." she had started to explain, but he cut her words short.

"Don't think," he'd told her harshly. "It just causes trouble."

As she drove along, she wondered why she'd ever married Anthony. At first, she refused to admit even to herself that she'd made a mistake, but after two years, after Anthony had actually struck her for not carrying out some order explicitly, she realized that her young and foolish dreams of happily-ever-after had been wishful thinking. He had charmed her with his attention, his self-confidence, his refined manners during their courtship.

And his money. She had to admit now that even that had influenced her when she accepted his proposal of marriage. She enjoyed having him send his limo and driver to pick her up, dining at the best restaurants where he was treated like royalty, the furs he insisted she buy.

But she soon discovered that his money was just that. His money. He gave her charge accounts at certain stores and at a certain beauty salon, but the allowance he gave her was smaller than the salary she made while employed at the Laurie Lee Cosmetic Company where they met when he came to buy a gift for his mother.

How sweet, she thought at the time, and only later learned that he stopped to make his purchase when he spotted her talking to a customer as he made his way through the store.

He'd been intrigued by her, he admitted later. He thought she was not only a rare beauty, but that her attitude of deference, but not fawning, showed old fashioned courtesy to him as a customer. He liked that, and she liked his approval, not realizing that his affable and gracious behavior was meant to appeal to her.

At least one good thing came from her marriage. She gave a quick glance to the back seat where Amanda lay sleeping, damp dark curls making ringlets across her forehead. Mandy. She was Elaine's world. She'd do anything to keep her from being raised in the cold atmosphere of Anthony's house, to keep her from being influenced by her father's philosophy toward fellow human beings.

And Aaron. She liked to think she'd brought a little joy into his young life. He'd been three when she married his father. Elaine took him to her heart on those occasions when he was allowed to visit.

After learning he wasn't to be a part of their home she eventually arranged to pick him up at his grandmother's without asking for Anthony's permission. If he knew or minded, he never said so. Most of the time he ignored her and the children.

Certainly Aaron's grandmother didn't care. A tall, perfectly groomed woman, an older feminine version of her son, she always seemed to be more concerned with her clubs and parties than the care of her grandson. His physical needs were met by servants hired for that purpose, but his grandmother merely tolerated him, and was as cold and aloof to him as to Elaine.

One time Elaine had been told to go to Aaron's grandmother's to get him. A servant let her in and told her which room Aaron was in. She went up the long polished stairs to the room indicated. She found it magnificent. Aaron had his own television, a computer, radio, clock, shelves of books and games and toys. There was a closet filled with clothes. It was decorated in cheery colors.

But Aaron never looked happy. The fact that he was not an untroubled, carefree child was reflected in his sad, dark eyes.

On occasional visits to his father's house she tried to do fun things that she hoped he might enjoy. Together they played games he'd never heard of. Sometimes she took both he and Amanda to the zoo even though Amanda was still too small to appreciate the outing. But Elaine could never bear the thought of leaving her alone at the house in the sterile care of any of Anthony's employees.

Aaron adored Amanda. When she was born he would sit beside her, letting her fingers curl around one of his while an expression of rapture would brighten his face.

"My little sister," he would say, and after a time he got so he would give her rosy cheek a kiss.

In the beginning Aaron never showed any affection to her or to his father, but when Elaine started giving him a quick kiss and a gentle pat on the shoulder at the end of each visit, he eventually accepted such gestures casually and even initiated them sometimes.

She watched him now, chattering away, a far cry from the shy, withdrawn boy whom she first met.

All day the sardonic, smiling face of Martin Sills had hovered over her like a bad omen. He would have liked to have interfered earlier that morning when she said she was going to pick up her car that the man from the garage had taken in for servicing.

"I'll get it for you when it's done," he'd told her.

"I may not want to wait that long. I have plans for the day," she'd answered, trying to keep her tone light and unconcerned, yet firm in intent.

"Things to do?" A cigarette dangled from Sill's thin smiling lips. Bright blue eyes never quit moving above a hawk-like nose. She was sure it was his job to keep an eye on her, to see what she did, where she went, whom she saw, and to report it all to Anthony.

"You might say so." She patted back a mock yawn.

"Want me to drive you to the garage?"

"I've already called a cab."

"You must be in a hurry?"

She ignored that remark to gather up Amanda and head out the door, saying only, "Here it is now."

She had been pacing the floor all morning, worrying that the service man might open the trunk and find all the things she had packed in there. If he did, would he call Anthony at his office? Would Anthony come tearing across the city to forcibly stop her from leaving? Or would he send Sills to detain her until he could get there?

As she got out of the cab she was relieved to find her car still parked over at one side, but her relief immediately disappeared when she saw Sills leaning against Anthony's Cadillac. How had he got here so quickly? And why?

He strolled ever so casually toward her.

She walked past him without speaking.

"I need the car now," she told the attendant. "You can service it later."

Sills followed beside her.

"How come you need it in such a hurry?" He smirked. His eyes never quit moving, they seemed to always be watching every direction at once. He would delight in getting something on her to report to Anthony. He disliked her and never pretended otherwise. She considered the feeling to be mutual.

"I have plans for the day," she answered, trying to appear unconcerned. "I promised the kids we'd go to the zoo and eat out." She strapped Amanda into her car seat. She got in behind the steering wheel and shut the door, one hand on the window button.

"Oh. I thought maybe you had business that was taking you out of town?"

You wish, she thought. She only said, "Has Anthony instructed you to mind my business?" She shot the window up to the top and started the motor, trying to keep each movement she made to appear unhurried.

She saw his mouth form the words, "Not yet," before she headed out of the parking lot.

She would not leave without telling Aaron goodbye. That would be cruel. Hopefully, if Sills followed, he would think she was stopping to get Aaron for the day's outing she'd just mentioned. She had no thought at that time of taking Aaron with her, but when she told him she was leaving Chicago to go to southern Iowa, she was torn by his grief at the thought of her and Mandy leaving.

"Please, Laine," he'd begged, using his shortened version of her name. "Don't leave." Tears filled his eyes.

"I must, Aaron. I can't take it here anymore."

"Take me with you, Laine." He held onto her as she stood outside her car parked in his grandmother's driveway. "Father doesn't like me. He told me he didn't. He says I remind him of my mother, and he hates my mother."

"Oh, Aaron." Her heart went out to the boy, but she was too concerned for Amanda's welfare to stay.

"Grandmother doesn't like me either. She says I'm a bother. Don't leave me, Laine. I can't bear it here without you and Mandy." He wrapped his thin arms around Elaine's waist.

"Oh, Aaron, I wish I could take you, but you know your father will never allow you to go." She didn't think he would allow Amanda to go, either. That wasn't Anthony's way. What was his, was his.

"I'm afraid, Laine. Please. I told you what I saw that last night that I stayed at Father's house."

Elaine hadn't forgotten. She wasn't sure she believed Aaron's story, even though she had long suspected that her husband's business deals were sometimes of an unsavory nature. But murder?

"Now, Aaron," she spoke gently, cajolingly. "Maybe you can come visit me and Amanda when we get settled." That was an empty promise. Anthony would never allow him to go, in fact, she was almost certain that he would sue to get Mandy back. Her only hope to keep her daughter would be to fight it out in court. She needed Emma's support, her wisdom in just how to go about such things.

She walked out to her car, carrying Amanda, and with Aaron following close behind, purportedly just telling her good-bye for the day, for if Grandmother learned of anything different, that news would be certain to reach Anthony at once.

"You mustn't tell your grandmother that I'm leaving for good, Aaron."

"I'll die if I can't go with you, Laine," he whispered intensely. "Father's mean." He looked around to make certain that no one was within earshot. "If I stay, he might tell Martin to kill me, too."

"Oh, Aaron, that's foolish nonsense. Your father would never do something like that. You're his son."

"He hates me. And he hated my mother. He won't ever talk about her, nor Grandmother either. Maybe he killed her, too, like he did the man in the library."

"Oh, Aaron . . ."

"I'm not lying. The man was awfully quiet. I know he was dead. It was Roger Reams. Martin saw me and said, 'Can it. It's the boy'." Aaron deepened his voice and frowned menacingly, mocking Sills. "Father looked really angry. He walked right past me when he came out of the library. He never said a word to me, but he told Martin, 'Take care of him, Sills'. I think he wanted Martin to get rid of me, too."

"But that doesn't mean . . ."

Aaron was nodding his head for emphasis, his eyes had a far-away look. "Martin grabbed hold of my shoulder, and he was grinnin', you know." Aaron mimicked Sill's cynical smile. "Martin said, 'Trust me, Mr. Bradbury.' And he kept real tight hold of me 'til he got me in his car and drove me back to Grandmother's. On the way, he tried to tell me that Mr. Reams was sleeping. I told him I knew it." His voice sank to a deeper whisper as he added, "I'm not dumb."

"Are you sure it was Mr. Reams?"

He nodded. "I've seen him with Father before. You're the only one who really cares about me, Laine. I'm afraid Martin will kill me, too."

"Come now, Aaron, I hardly think . . ." Surely Anthony wouldn't harm his own son, she told herself. She didn't doubt that Sills was capable of even worse things. Dare she go and leave Aaron here?

"Last night," Aaron's voice dropped to little more than a whisper, "when Martin dropped me off here at Grandmother's, he parked across the street. I got out of the car to walk across, and he started up real quick. He almost hit me."

What could she do? Anthony would never allow her to take Aaron legally. He wasn't her child . . . wasn't her responsibility. But suppose Aaron was telling her the absolute truth and had reason to be afraid?

"Oh, there's Martin now." Aaron ducked down as his father's shiny black automobile swung around the corner of the next street and came toward them. Elaine ignored him, but Aaron, his face white, opened her door and crawled behind her seat and into the back.

Sills smirked as he passed them to turn into Mrs. Bradbury's driveway. Evidently he didn't see Aaron and presumed she was parked in the street waiting for him to come out so they could go to the zoo like she'd said.

Almost without thinking Elaine put her car into motion and pulled away from the curb and down the street. Aaron's grandmother wasn't home, she knew. Hopefully, the servants would assume she'd been allowed to take Aaron for the day and Sills would not follow her. If he didn't, she might have time to get the children out of the city and into Iowa before Anthony realized she was gone.

She'd even pulled into a parking space near the zoo entrance, and sat there in the car for awhile, watching carefully for some sign of Sills. Seeing none, she headed south, taking main streets out of Chicago and hoping her car would blend in with the traffic.

Now, here she was hours later, still worried. Her eyes continually searched the rearview mirror for indication that she was being followed.

A green and white sign ahead indicated that they were only a few miles from Fulton Falls. No drive at all if she felt fresh, but after a sleepless night, her increasing weariness gave reason to look for a motel once they reached Fulton Falls. She didn't anticipate the idea of driving over unknown country roads in the dark in search of a place she'd never seen before. Surely Fulton Falls would offer food and lodging. She was tired and so were the children. Aaron was fighting sleep, and Amanda was turning restlessly in the confinement of her car seat in an attempt to stretch out.

She could call Emma from a motel and let her know they wouldn't be arriving until the following day.

She turned into the first motel she saw, the bright light beckoning her in. She struggled to carry Amanda's limp body. Aaron needed only a nudge to bring him awake. She looked with disappointment at the sign that said the dining room was closed.

"There's an all night diner just down the street," the clerk at the desk told her, seeing her let-down expression as she read the sign.

She placed two twenty dollar bills next to the ledger on the counter. "Could I get you to run and get us some soup and sandwiches . . . or whatever they have and bring it to our room?"

He folded the bills and put them in his pocket.

"Sure thing. I'll have it to you in just a few minutes."

He did. Even Amanda was revived by the aroma of the hamburgers, and the soup which they ate with plastic spoons from paper cups.

"Baths and bed," Elaine announced when they finished.

"But, Laine, I haven't any pajamas," Aaron protested hopefully.

"No matter. You can sleep in your shorts and T-shirt. We'll stop tomorrow and buy you some stuff."

After her own shower, she stood looking down at Aaron who had curled into a ball in the center of one of the double beds, his hands doubled into two fists. He looked so small, so defenseless that even though she doubted her wisdom in bringing him along, she couldn't be sorry. How could she have left him at the mercy of a man like Sills?

Taking Amanda and running might not be without ramifications, but as of yet she had as much right to have her as had Anthony. There had been no court hearing granting guardianship to either of them.

With Aaron, she'd actually committed a crime. She had no doubt that Anthony would use that as a weapon against her. Kidnapping was a serious offense even if it was a real parent who made off with his own child without having been granted custody.

A sick feeling hit her in the pit of her stomach. Would a judge regard her actions as wrong and thereby influence any decision made about Amanda should Anthony seek sole custody?

She trembled as she lay her head down on the pillow next to Amanda who was already asleep in the other bed.

"Oh, Mandy, what have I done?" she cried silently as realization sank in with a final, awful condemnation.

She'd call Emma. A glance at the clock showed her it was after ten. Emma would still be up, surely.

Taking her cell phone from her jacket pocket she carried

it over to a chair, sank down with her head back against the soft cushion, and started to dial when she was struck by a sudden thought: *Was there some way that Anthony would be able to trace her whereabouts through cell phone records?*

She put it aside and picked up the motel phone from the dresser top and dialed the number.

Chapter Three

Emma's greeting was so warm, so filled with sympathy over the phone that Elaine was almost reduced to tears. Her friend's encouraging words cracked the shield of righteous indignation she'd used to deny even to herself that what she did was wrong. Criminally wrong.

"I was just getting ready to start worrying," Emma said with a little laugh. "Where are you?"

Elaine swallowed hard, clearing her aching throat. What would Emma say when she heard the whole story?

"Parkview Motel on Highway 34. I'm just too tired to drive on in. And the kids are worn out. It's getting late and I'm afraid I might have a hard time finding your place."

"The kids?"

"Mandy and Aaron. And I need to run in to a store and pick up a few things for him."

"Aaron?

"You know Aaron. My stepson."

There was a short silence. "Of course I know who Aaron is. I just wasn't aware that he was coming with you."

"He's not supposed to be with me. Anthony doesn't know I brought him." She hated telling Emma and added with false heartiness, "At least I hope he doesn't know yet."

Following an even longer silence, Emma said, "Maybe you'd better tell me what's going on."

Elaine decided not to mention what Aaron said about Mr. Reams. Not yet, anyway. "I felt so sorry for him, Emma. He's s-so neglected . . . oh, not through care, but he hasn't got anyone to love him. No one cares two cents about what happens to him. Not really."

"Oh, Elaine. Really."

"He's such a sweet boy, Emma. I know you. You'd have done the same thing in my place. When I told him that Mandy and I were leaving, he begged to come along. Anthony has almost nothing to do with him, and his grandmother barely tolerates him."

"And Anthony doesn't know he's with you?"

"I didn't tell him."

"That's kidnapping, Elaine."

If Emma thought her actions were that serious, then they must be. "I just acted on the spur of the moment. I don't know why I did, but I don't know how I could have left him either . . . under the circumstances."

"And how long, dear child, do you think it will take for your husband to figure out where you've gone? He knows you and I are friends. Don't you suppose he'll think of me right off?"

"I know," Elaine admitted miserably. "I'll have to go somewhere else."

"Oh, Elaine, I don't mean to be critical, but surely you didn't stop and weigh the consequences."

Elaine caught her lower lip between her teeth. "It seemed like the right thing to do at the time. And . . . and you don't know everything yet."

"There's more?"

"I'd rather explain further when I get there. Maybe you can help me decide what to do . . . where to go. I never thought about causing you trouble, Emma. Or implicating you."

"Never mind me. It's Laurie Lee I'm thinking about."

"Yes, of course. We can rest a bit, maybe, and then go on to . . ."

She couldn't think of anyplace to go on to. No place where she and the children would be safe.

She had no family, no friends other than Emma. There was Lyle Shubin of course, but she could never ask him for help. Lyle wanted to be more than friends when they both worked for the Laurie Lee Cosmetic Company. He was a decent sort, hard working and steady, but he was the kind who never took chances, who would never be involved in a crime.

To ensure that he wouldn't become worried about her, she had telephoned him that morning before leaving the house.

"Leaving? Well, I can't say that I blame you. I don't know how you've stayed with that man this long. Where are you going?" His voice was gentle and sympathetic and she visualized how warm and concerned his brown eyes would be if she was talking to him in person.

"I'd rather not say, Lyle. But I wanted you to know so you wouldn't worry."

"Anthony doesn't know?"

"No. And don't tell him anything . . . especially that I called you. I want to get Amanda away from him before he finds out I'm gone."

"I doubt I see him. I never do. I'm not exactly in his circle, you know."

"I know. But you were at one of his parties."

"Because of you. That was the only reason I was invited. Promise me you'll call me when you get settled."

"I will."

But that conversation, she remembered, had taken place before she decided to include Aaron in her flight.

Emma's voice cut in on her reverie. "We'll discuss all that at another time. I'm sure we can sort things out."

"I know it's an imposition for you and Laurie Lee . . . I mean Miss Randall."

"We'll cross that bridge later. She isn't even home right now. I just don't want the media to get wind of this and make an issue of what you did. You know how they are. Laurie Lee hates bad publicity."

"I know. You've told me."

Emma gave a little laugh. "Nothing must threaten her image," she warned. "We'll just keep quiet until we can decide what to do."

Elaine wished Emma would quit saying "what you did" in that tone of voice. But there was no denying how wrong she'd been in bringing Aaron with her.

"Mum's the word," Elaine agreed.

"I know people in California," Emma said thoughtfully. "We'll work out something."

"That should be far enough away," Elaine answered.

But was it far enough to keep away from Anthony? Hadn't he once calmly told her he'd go to the ends of the earth to get even with anyone who crossed him?

"Maybe we can get you on at the distribution center in Los Angeles. You were an employee in good standing when you left to marry Anthony, weren't you?"

"Yes. Will Laur . . . Miss Randall remember me?"

Emma's answer was hesitant. "I doubt it. You were just one of hundreds that worked for her."

Elaine could recall numerous times she watched the lovely Laurie Lee flit airly in and out of the lobby on her way to plush offices on an upper floor. Sometimes it seemed that her employer seemed to float—her step was light and graceful. She made Elaine think of a butterfly in her bright colors. Her dark hair shone and her skin glowed with health and vitality and with Laurie Lee Cosmetics.

As always, somewhere on her person, either in her hair, or as a pin on a lapel, or maybe at the end of a chain around her neck was the symbol of her business, the company logo, a bright green feather.

The pin was green and gold and curled slightly upward at the end. Sometimes the symbol showed up in delicate earrings shaped like tiny green feathers, or made up into a bracelet of small feathers of jade, wreathed together and mounted on a gold band.

Emma's voice became softer, with a whisper of conspiracy.

"Do you suppose we could introduce you by a different name? If Laurie Lee comes home while you're still here, maybe she'll never have to know what you got involved in . . . who you really are . . . until we get you on a plane to California. How about using your maiden name? Webster? Tell Aaron."

"Of course. I'll caution him about everything. And I'm sorry about getting you involved."

So now she was going to use an alias. Did doing one wrong deed allow the justification of doing another?

"Let's say no more about this now," Emma said. "Wait until you get here. I'm anxious to see Amanda. And you. I haven't seen you since I visited you that one time after she was born. How long's that been?"

"Amanda's three now. Pretty as a picture."

"And I expect you've painted lots of those of her."

"Pictures? Oh, yes."

"They'll make you rich and famous some day."

"Don't I wish?"

"You're good. You gave me one the day I stopped to tell you good-bye before I moved down here. Remember?"

"But that one was of Aaron, not Amanda."

"Has he changed much?"

"He's taller. He's ten now, going on eleven."

"I told Mitch that you were coming. You and Amanda."

"How is Mitch?"

"He's a good-looking kid." She laughed. "Listen to me.

You'd think he was a teenager instead of almost thirty. He manages the farm for Laurie Lee."

"Manager? I'm impressed."

Emma's laugh reminded her of the old carefree Emma that she always liked. "Well, considering there are only five or six working under him, he'd say it isn't too impressive."

"Sounds good to me." Elaine was glad Emma was in a better mood again.

"He's doing okay. The pheasant business has prospered since he took over. We'll have a hatch in a few days."

"The kids will enjoy that."

"I'm looking forward to seeing you in the morning."

As she hung up the phone Elaine had the uneasy feeling that Emma wasn't as enthusiastic about her arrival as when she first issued the invitation.

She turned out the light and lay down beside Amanda, being careful not to awaken her as she stretched her tired, aching body out between the clean cool sheets. She was so weary she supposed she would go to sleep immediately, but she kept going back over the events of the day, and worrying if Sills could have followed her out here.

She kept remembering, too, the day Emma first issued the invitation to visit her at Laurie Lee's farm at Fulton Falls. *Had that been a mere week ago?* How much longer it seemed.

Elaine had considered the invitation doubtfully. *A guest in Laurie Lee's house?* She protested, but Emma remained unruffled.

"I don't think I should do that," she said hesitantly.

"Nonsense." Emma had dismissed her arguments. "Laurie Lee never troubles herself about whom I ask to visit. When I agreed to work here she said I was to consider this my home, not just a place of employment. We've been friends for years, long before she was my employer. I can't wait to see how Amanda has changed. You're not telling Anthony you're leaving, are you?" Of course, at the time,

Emma nor Elaine herself for that matter, knew Aaron would be along. Making off with Amanda presented a large enough problem, but by taking Aaron it had become gigantic.

"Definitely not," she'd answered, and immediately started planning how she could leave without antagonizing Anthony. Everyone would be better off if she never even told him she was leaving him. She'd tried broaching the subject of divorce once last winter, and never mentioned it again. He had eyed her dispassionately, looking more annoyed than anything.

"You may go anytime you wish, Elaine," he said, "but don't even dream of taking Amanda."

"I'd never leave without Amanda," she told him. The very thought of leaving her beautiful, innocent little daughter to Anthony's cold-blooded care made her sick to her stomach.

"You'll never take her with you," he assured her callously. "I promise you that."

What chance would she have by going to court? He had influential friends and acquaintances. Judges and lawyers moved in the same circle as he did. Anthony's power talked and his money kept others from talking.

So she'd bided her time, saving all the cash she could from her allowance, carefully carrying out clothing, and storing one article at a time in her locker at the gym. She'd deliberately started working out so as to have just such a hiding place. She would wear sweaters out of the house when it was warm, and never wear them back in. She took her good coat and several pantsuits to the cleaners and left them there until the day before her departure.

Amanda flung an arm across her face, and murmured, "Mama," in her sleep. Elaine gently placed it back by her side. She willed herself to sleep, too, and finally drifted off silently repeating a favorite saying of her foster father's. "Act in haste, and repent in leisure."

She had plenty of leisure time now. Plenty of time to repent.

She rolled and tossed, dreaming she was being sent to prison for what she'd done. She'd cried and pleaded for the authorities to bring Amanda back to her, but no one would listen. Anthony turned away from her in the dream with a cold smile on his face and said, "Take care of her, Sills." And no matter how far she ran, Sills kept following her, kept smiling his sardonic smile as if he were visualizing what he would do with her once he caught up.

Chapter Four

The sun was shining through the motel window when Elaine awoke the next morning. Rested and eager to be on her way, and knowing that her friend was near, nothing looked as hopeless as it had the night before.

"All's right with the world," she murmured as she stepped out of the shower. Surely when Anthony realized that Aaron was happy and safe with her, he would not press charges. Hopefully, she would be able to negotiate with him to keep Aaron if she agreed to give up child support for Amanda.

Reality hit her. Her shoulders sagged.

And maybe the moon truly was made of green cheese. One idea was about as likely as the other. *Of what use to Anthony would be the paltry sum she might be awarded for support? Who was she fooling?*

There was no turning back. Now she must rise or fall with the consequences. She didn't regret bringing Aaron. Years of pity had changed into caring for him, for his welfare. Sorrow for his neglect, for the lack of love in his life made her determined to better his world.

After hearing his story she was afraid that if she didn't step in, his very life might be in danger. She found it hard to believe, but what if it was all true? The fear that he was relating exactly what he saw was very compelling. His love and trust provided her with the incentive needed to stay on the path she'd started.

"Mama," came a voice from the bed.

Amanda was sitting up, her chubby hands, dimpled into fists, were rubbing the sleep out of her heavy-lidded eyes. Aaron came awake, too, blinking rapidly as he hopped out of bed, aware all at once of where he was.

"Good morning, Aaron," she said, deliberately cheerful.

He pulled on his pants and shirt. "I've never slept in a motel before," he told her, wonder in his voice. He ran around the room, looking out every window and marveling at the cars and delivery trucks rushing by.

She tousled his hair. "You've got a lot of firsts in store for you," she said optimistically, and thought, *you've never been kidnapped before, either.*

Amanda tumbled out from under the blankets and toddled over to her, arms up, sleepy-eyed, wanting to be cuddled.

"Are you hungry?" Elaine crooned, sitting down with her on the side of the bed and rocking back and forth, the child cradled in her arms.

Amanda nodded. "I'se hungry."

"Me, too," Aaron said. "I can eat a whole stack of pancakes." He zipped around the room, looking out the windows while Elaine got Amanda and then herself dressed.

They left the motel, walking down the block toward the restaurant that was advertised on a flyer on the motel desk, The Circle Inn, a tall building made of brick and stone.

Amanda skipped along between them, one hand hanging onto Elaine's, while Aaron held on to her other one.

From a distance church bells tolled, bringing a sense of peace, and calming Elaine's nervousness.

Inside they found that steps led down a short flight of stairs to a room designated as "The Cellar" where a sign was posted at the top of the stairs stating, BREAKFAST SERVED IN THE CELLAR. They went down. A hostess showed them to a small table in the center of the room.

Aaron's eyes sparkled with excitement. "Look," he said, and pointed upward. From where they sat they could see all the way up to floors on the upper levels through a huge circular opening in each floor, each ringed by a railing of wood and wrought iron for safety.

"I want to go up there," Aaron said, and jumped up excitedly.

"Oh, no, you're not," she said firmly, and pulled him back down to his chair. "You're staying right here. They serve breakfast here."

She tipped her head back to look up, then looked away instantly. Heights did that to her—made her stomach flip-flop when she looked down from a distance. And even when looking up, she visualized looking down.

"I'd like to see down from up there," he persisted, head still thrown back.

She shivered. "I wouldn't. How about those pancakes?" She scanned the menu.

"Can-pakes," Amanda agreed from her high chair.

"Could we just go up and look down?" Aaron begged after his stack of cakes were gone. Against her better judgment, she agreed, provided both children promised to hold her hands.

They climbed the winding stairs to the second floor. A brass plaque on the wall near the bottom step stated that the structure had once been a government building, now remodeled, preserving as much historic atmosphere as possible.

"Hang on to my hand, Aaron," Elaine reminded as he pulled away to run ahead a few steps.

"I'm not afraid." He marched ahead.

"But I am," Elaine told him, one of Amanda's hands gripped tightly in one of her own.

Instantly, Aaron was by her side. ·

"Don't hang onto the railing," she cautioned. "Stand back."

"This is great," Aaron enthused, peering down.

Elaine turned abruptly away. "Let's go." Still hanging onto Amanda she reached a hand out for Aaron just as a group of people surged up the stairs and pressed forward. She tried to back away as the crowd, talking and laughing, and not knowing her unrealistic fright, jammed her closer to the railing. She looked down in spite of her determination not to. Her stomach heaved. She was light-headed and dizzy.

She shook. How easy it would be for someone to be pushed over the railing. It could happen if someone was caught off balance. What if Sills was in this crowd? Who would notice if he gave her a quick, hard shove?

She kept thrusting herself back into the throng, Amanda up in her arms. "Aaron, stay with me," she said shrilly. As quickly as the mass gathered, it dispersed just as fast, leaving only a few people by the railing.

"Let's get out of here." She knew it was ridiculous to be this nervous, but she couldn't help it. Her legs were weak and trembling. "We're taking the elevator," she declared.

She led the way out of the store and up the street where she'd spotted a clothing store. She bought Aaron a few things before hurrying them back to the motel where she got their luggage into the car and headed once more down the highway.

"We're almost there," she sang out later, turning off the highway to follow the directions that Emma gave her. "Now, be on your best behavior."

Laurie Lee Randall's house was set back from the road, sprawling out in two directions. It appeared to Elaine to be made mostly of brick and wood and fronted by a long porch. Rows of pine trees and blue spruce bordered the yard on one side and formed a grove at the back.

A neatly trimmed white fence sparkled in the sunlight at the back and the other side of the yard.

Elaine followed the pine-bordered drive that circled around the house. Pulling up at one side, she braked to a stop and turned off the engine. Before she could even set one foot out of the car, a tall woman with white hair came hurrying down the walk to meet them.

"Emma," Elaine cried joyfully. Happiness at seeing her friend now supplanted her doubt as to how Emma might react that she had an extra person along. She basked in the warm hug that Emma gave her and thought that this must be how it feels to come home.

"So good to see you, Elaine," Emma greeted her enthusiastically. She opened the car door and took Amanda out of her car seat, holding her up for a close inspection. Amanda wiggled to get down.

"Oh, Elaine. She's absolutely lovely. She has your eyes."

"And this is Aaron." Elaine drew Aaron forward.

Emma stood Amanda down and offered Aaron her hand. "I'm glad to see you again, Aaron," she said. Aaron studied her gravely for a minute before slipping his hand into hers, "He and Amanda do look a little alike, don't they?"

"I guess so. Yes." Elaine hated to admit that either of them could favor their father. She opened the trunk and began removing boxes and paper bags.

"Love your luggage," Emma commented dryly, looking amused.

"I sort of kept my departure secret," Elaine explained ruefully and shrugged her shoulders.

"Serves the purpose," Emma declared airily. She picked up a couple of the boxes, while Aaron lugged a bag and Elaine carried the rest.

They trooped into the house, following Emma across the entry and down a long hall. Leading up from the hall was a long elegant stairway, the oak wood gleaming with polish, the steps carpeted.

Emma paused by the first door at the head of the stairs. "This is my room," she said. "Mitch's room is down there at the end. I'm putting you and the children across from me. Here." She opened a door to let Elaine and the children enter a large high-ceilinged room.

Several windows on both sides of the room let in the morning light. A vase of fresh cut flowers stood on a table in front of the windows.

"Emma, how nice." Elaine deposited her boxes on the bed and smiled in appreciation.

Emma opened a connecting door on the far side of the room. "This room will be Aaron's. I'll have Veronica put up a cot in your room for Amanda."

"That's fine," Elaine said gratefully. She was sure the small room off her own had been intended for Amanda, but not by word or sign did Emma indicate that the plans she made were not being carried out explicitly.

Emma opened another door and showed Elaine a bathroom done in white and lavender. The wall was papered, the pattern was of ivy mingled with tiny white flowers. Fluffy white carpet covered the bathroom floor. Two hanging baskets of green ivy hung near a huge mirror.

"You can unpack later," Emma said. "Let's go down and have something cool to drink."

She led the way back down the stairs and out onto a screened porch at the back. Emma sat down, motioning for Elaine to sit in a tall wicker chair next to the one she sat in. Aaron took Amanda by the hand and led her out to tumble about on the grassy yard.

Emma sighed. "I tell you, Elaine, that after all those hectic years I spent in the business world, working here for Laurie Lee is pure joy."

"That's easy to imagine," Elaine responded, and yet couldn't imagine it.

A woman, plumpish, with faded blond hair pulled back

to the nape of her neck, came out the back door carrying a tray of lemonade.

"This is Pauline Page, Elaine," Emma introduced them. "Better known as Polly. Polly, this is my friend, Elaine . . . Webster, and her children, Aaron and Amanda."

"Pleased to meet you," Pauline said politely. "I hope you enjoy your visit with us." She smiled as she left, stopping only to plump up some cushions on a glider as she made her way back inside.

Moments later she was back, carrying salads on a tray. She arranged the plates on the glass-topped table, setting out cruets of various dressings and a glass dish filled with crackers.

"Anything else, Emma?" Pauline asked, as she helped Amanda up to the table, putting a thick cushion under her so she could reach her plate better.

"I don't think so, Polly." Emma smiled at her.

After lunch Emma took them on a tour of the farm, meeting several workers along the way. She stopped to introduce a young woman with fly-away hair and dark angry eyes who was washing the outside windows on the lower floor.

"This is Veronica Meeks, Elaine. Veronica, Elaine Webster. Elaine's an old friend. She's visiting us for a few days or so. And these are her children, Aaron and Amanda."

The girl turned resentful eyes on them. She nodded to Elaine, and gazed sourly at the children. Elaine made a mental note to remind Aaron and Amanda to keep their fingerprints off the glass.

"Veronica is married to Irving," Emma explained. "Irving is Laurie Lee's cousin. They both work here."

At six o'clock, Mitchell joined them for the evening meal. He smiled at her as he came in the family dining room. He was dressed in tan slacks, leaving his shirt open at the neck. He went to her immediately, one hand outstretched.

"Nice to see you again," he said. "Mother's been anxious for you to get here." His smile broadened. He regarded her quizzically. "You don't remember me, do you?"

"Oh, yes, I do. But you were gone quite a lot those times I spent at your mother's." And from the moment Anthony started his calculated courtship of her she had eyes for no one else. "You look like your mother."

"Poor mother," he said, and turned his attention to Amanda and Aaron.

He resembled Emma: his hair the color of ripened wheat, was once that of his mother's, his eyes, a piercing blue, were Emma's, too.

The children ate with them. Pauline had fixed steaks, grilled with garlic butter, wild rice, squash and green beans. Dessert was glazed, bright red strawberries heaped in crystal bowls with a dollop of whipped topping.

"My goodness, Emma," Elaine said, as they got up from the table. "How do you keep so thin?"

"The eternal struggle," Emma sighed.

"And running her legs off for Madame Lee."

"Mitchell." Emma frowned at her son.

"Sorry." He threw his napkin down by his plate. "Pay no attention to me, Elaine. Mother still has to wash out my mouth sometimes."

After the meal was over they all strolled out to the back porch and the yard.

"I hear you're a manager now." Elaine sat down on a wicker chair.

"Mother." He sent a chiding look at Emma who was lying back on a lounge.

"Somebody's got to toot your horn," she replied calmly, relaxed. She never opened her eyes.

"I'm just the manager of the farm. A farmer."

"Oh, a bit more than that," Emma disagreed casually.

"A pheasant farm." Elaine said pleasantly, but her thoughts were back in Chicago, wondering what Anthony was doing about her disappearance. She had no illusions about his anger, but just what he would do to put things back in his control was the cause for her doubts. "I always thought of pheasants as wild birds."

"Well, they're not too tame sometimes," Mitchell admitted, still standing, watching Aaron and Amanda play. "In fact, the ones we sell aren't tame at all."

"Sounds interesting." She tried to keep her mind on the conversation. "I'm anxious to see them. I'm sure Aaron and Amanda would like to see them, too."

"Tomorrow," Mitchell promised. He smiled down at Aaron who had left off playing at the sound of his name. "Would you and your sister like to go with your mother and me to see the pheasants tomorrow?"

Aaron's eyes flickered, and Elaine held her breath as she waited to see how the boy would handle Mitchell calling her his mother. There hadn't been a chance to warn him yet.

"That would be fun," Aaron answered simply, after sending her a quick glance.

"Do they look like all the pictures I've seen of pheasants?" Elaine wondered, heaving a sigh of relief and wanting to turn his attention away from their supposed relationship.

"You're probably thinking of the ring-necked. We have other breeds, too. But one thing I want you and your sister to remember, Aaron, never go in the pens by yourself. The roosters have very sharp spurs."

"Very wicked." Emma had opened her eyes and was sitting up.

"Sometimes they get really riled up," Mitchell continued sternly. "So promise you'll never go in the pens by yourselves."

"I promise," Aaron said solemnly, and Amanda ducked her head in shy agreement.

"That's where the green feather symbol on all of the Laurie Lee products originated," Emma reminded her.

"Of course." Elaine remembered. "When I worked there I saw the green feather on everything, but I guess I was thinking more in terms of the legend she used in advertising." She always thought the green feather symbol was attractive. Embossed above the script, 'Laurie Lee,' the feather seemed to float above the written words.

A man appeared at the corner of the house. "I'm ready when you are, Mitch."

"Got to go," Mitchell said. "See you all tomorrow."

"How late do they work?" Elaine wondered.

"He and Irving have been putting in long hours, cleaning out pens, getting ready for new chicks."

"Irving?"

"The man who was just here. He's Laurie Lee's cousin."

The man married to the sullen woman she'd met earlier.

Later, as they got ready to go to bed, Emma handed each of them a clear plastic packet. "Every overnight guest gets a pack of Laurie Lee products," she said.

After the children were asleep, Elaine showered with Laurie Lee body wash, shampooed with Laurie Lee shampoo, and used all the appropriate cleansers and moisturizers. Wide awake, she sank into a chair by the upstairs window, and turned out the light so as not to bother Amanda. She gazed out at the darkened surroundings.

The moon shone down, and the wind blew through the oak trees. She leaned on the windowsill and looked out.

What had happened to her life that she once supposed would be orderly and happy? What had happened to the dreams that she'd dreamed? The plans she once made concerning her future? How had she got caught up in this situation?

Surely Anthony wouldn't care enough to come looking for them, she mused. *Might he just send Sills to see if this is where she had fled to two days ago?*

So many people were here on the farm who would surely come to her aid should Anthony or his hoodlum worker come here with the intention of taking Amanda and her brother.

This was such a beautiful place. She felt safe, yet she couldn't help wondering, *were the children safe anywhere?*

Chapter Five

When Elaine woke up the next morning the horizon was black with storm clouds tumbling across the southern and western sky. The wind blew in gusts unusually cool for June. A fine mist filled the air between the house and the pine trees. By mid-morning the sky was gray and the mist had given way to a drizzle, and later the drizzle became hard, downpouring rain.

The children dawdled around, discontent and bored. Elaine attempted to interest them in games, but Amanda was too young, and Aaron kept wanting to go out to see the pheasants.

"Let's have a wiener roast," Emma suggested. "A fire in the fireplace will help take the chill off. I've never seen a June so cool and damp."

"It'll change one of these days," Pauline predicted grimly, moving a lamp to dust a tabletop. "It'll turn off hot and humid, that's for sure." She nodded at the wisdom of her words, as if she alone was capable of knowing this and able to make such a forecast.

Emma smiled. "Well, you know what they say about Iowa . . . 'If you don't like the weather, stick around a day or two and it will change.' "

Emma, with the help of Pauline, soon had the fire blazing. "Tell you what," she said conspiratorially to the children, "after we get done with our wiener roast, I'll take you on a grand tour of the rest of the house. There are lots of paintings and beautiful porcelain sculptures that I'm sure your mother especially will enjoy."

Aaron sat down in front of the fireplace and watched the flames die down to smoldering coals. Emma handed him the big fork holding several hot dogs. Amanda sat close, watching him, the proud look on her face showing how much she admired her brother's know-how in roasting hot dogs. They sizzled and popped, filling the room with a smoky fragrance.

Pauline passed out plates of potato salad and baked beans.

"I like picnics," Amanda said in her shy, soft voice.

"Me, too," Emma responded. "Especially when there are no ants." They all laughed.

Mitchell came in.

"Now, this makes a perfect rainy day lunch." He smiled down at them while Emma filled his plate, and Aaron fixed him a hot dog. He carried it to the couch when he sat, hunched over the coffee table to eat.

"Emma's going to take us on a tour of the house," Aaron told him.

"A tour of the house, huh? Well, it's quite a place. One of my mother's great passions."

"And why not?" Emma retorted lightly. "How many people get the opportunity to live in a beautiful house like this? With someone as kind and thoughtful as Laurie Lee?"

He raised an eyebrow. "And have you told them the legend yet?"

"The legend?" Aaron was puzzled.

"A legend is a story," Elaine told him.

"Sure, there's a great legend behind Laurie Lee's success. You must get Mother to tell it to you." His eyes danced as he added, "Not that anyone can stop her from doing that. It's her favorite bedtime story."

Emma laughed. "Now, Mitch," she said fondly.

After lunch they carried the dishes into the kitchen.

"Now the tour," Emma told them, and led the way into the main part of the house.

They admired the living room with the high-beamed ceiling and soft lights and the Queen Anne furniture. In the formal dining room a polished mahogany table was centered under a crystal chandelier. Paintings hung on the wall and down the hallway. Thick carpet cushioned their feet. They climbed the open front stairs and looked into several guest rooms that were beautifully and tastefully furnished.

"I won't show you Laurie Lee's rooms," Emma said, passing by a closed door. "I'm sure when she gets home she will be happy to show you. Now, let's go through here. This door opens into the back hall toward our rooms. And here . . ." she led the way along the hall ". . . is the back stairs."

She led them into the library on the lower floor. There were shelves filled with books.

"Get something to read anytime you want," Emma told Elaine. "Laurie Lee says that's what they're for, and if someone doesn't read them, what good are they?"

"What about the legend?" Aaron hadn't forgotten.

"Okay, young man, let's go into the office over here and I'll tell you all the glorious details."

"Mitchell evidently doesn't think much of the legend," Elaine said. She remembered reading the story when she worked for Laurie Lee in Chicago, but she couldn't recall the details.

"Oh, Mitch." Emma dismissed her son's teasing with a wave of her hand. "Mitch is like a lot of men, sticklers for realism. Women like a little romance. Laurie Lee's business never boomed until she introduced the legend. Lots of times things like that can help. Why, I heard about someone who made cakes for sale, but never had much luck marketing them until she made up a legend to go with the cake. Fruit cakes, I think they were, and the legend was always printed on the inside lid of each box they were shipped in. She's very rich now."

"Just a story?" Aaron asked.

"I told you," Elaine responded.

Emma opened the door to Laurie Lee's office—which was decorated in an entirely different fashion. Plush green carpet covered the floor and the cream-colored walls were hung with bright tapestries consisting of rich fabrics artistically woven to create scenes of Indian folk lore. On her desk in a pottery vase were several pens fashioned like old quill pens, with long feathers of a brilliant green.

"All right, children, gather around," Emma told them. Her eyes sparkled with good humor. "Sit there on the floor and pretend the green carpet is grass and that you're back in ancient times." Emma sat down in a padded chair by the desk. Elaine found another place to sit as they all got ready to listen.

"Once upon a time . . ." she began.

Amanda's eyes danced. She clapped her chubby dimpled hands together. "Oh, I like this story," she chortled.

"Sh-h-h," Elaine warned.

Emma smiled good naturedly and started again. "Once upon a time there was a young Indian maiden . . .

"What's a maiden?" Aaron wondered.

"A young girl," Elaine answered. "Now hush and listen. No more interruptions."

"This Indian . . . girl was tall, and beautiful, and had long black hair that hung halfway down her back. All of the young men in her tribe would have liked to claim her hand in marriage, but they realized that she only had eyes for a young white man from a nearby village, and that he loved her, too. The Indian maiden's name was Green Feather.

"This young man was engaged to a lovely white girl

from his home state back East, long before he ever came out West with his future father-in-law. He intended to tell his fiancée about Green Feather, and ask her for a release from his commitment to her, but before he could tell her, his fiancée came West on a train for a surprise visit to both her father, who lived out there, and to her fiancé. She brought along her bridal finery so they could be married when she arrived.

"The young man wanted to tell her that he wanted to marry Green Feather, but he couldn't, for the day after her arrival her father was killed, and all of his holdings stolen. She was alone, entirely dependent on her fiancé with no means of supporting herself, and no money to go back East. She was helpless and frightened, stranded in a rough, unsettled land. He'd promised to care for her. His ring was on her finger.

"So this young man went to Green Feather and told her that even though he loved her, he must be true to his word. The Indian girl gave him a green feather as a sign of her undying love and vowed never to love anyone else, and never to forget him.

"The Indian girl went back to her people. She was sad and lonely and she counted off the days until his wedding by the rising and setting of the sun.

"The morning of the wedding she climbed barebacked on her mustang and rode like the wind, her long dark hair streaming out behind her. Her heart was bursting with sorrow as she listened to the ringing of the church bells proclaiming their wedding as she rode into town.

"When the couple came out of church and got into their carriage, there was a long green feather lying on the seat.

"The years passed, and they had a son. When the boy was old enough to start school he had to cross the river on a ferry, really not much more than a raft. Usually the current wasn't swift, but there had been a heavy rain and on that morning, the river was running high. A log hit the raft and broke it up. The man who ran the ferry saved himself, and tried to save the boy, but he couldn't.

"When the townspeople and the young couple reached the river they found the boy sitting on the bank near a hollow log, groggy but unhurt. On the ground beside him was a long, green feather. That was the last time the man saw any sign of the Indian girl. He felt that she must have drowned in the river saving his son."

"That's a good story," Aaron said. "Did Laurie Lee know her . . . Green Feather?"

"Hardly. Laurie Lee's not as old as I am." Emma laughed.

"That's a tale from many years ago," Elaine explained.

"And just a tale," Emma added, nodding her head in satisfaction at the retelling.

The following day, the children spent every moment that Elaine would allow out visiting the pheasants. Mitchell seemed pleased at their interest and walked with them from pen to pen, pointing out distinguishing marks in identifying the different breeds.

"The Reeves are my favorites," he told them. He opened a gate and entered a pen, closing it firmly behind him. He picked up a hen pheasant and held her close to the fence so they could see her better, rubbing a hand down her back to smooth out ruffled feathers.

"They're not mean, but they are touchy, so you mustn't ever come in alone. They can get stirred up if you frighten them."

"You handle them," Aaron pointed out.

"I guess you'd have to say that I know how. I've had a lot of experience these last few years."

"Can I learn how?" Aaron asked him, his expression serious. His eyes widened in anticipation.

"I don't see why not. When you're a little older."

Amanda hung back and wouldn't touch the hen, but

Aaron slipped his hand through the wire and touched her gently on her back.

"I'm not afraid," Aaron declared staunchly. "I'm gonna be an animal trainer someday."

"Well, I tell you, Aaron," Mitchell said easily without a hint of a smile, "there's not much demand for animal trainers around here." He set the hen on her feet and she fluttered over to the rest of the flock.

"How about being a veterinarian if you want to be around animals?" Elaine suggested.

"Yeah." Aaron welcomed that idea.

"Of course that takes a lot of schooling," Elaine added.

Aaron wrinkled his nose. "I knew there was a catch."

Later in the day when Elaine went to check on the children again she found the yard empty. She strolled out toward the pheasant pens.

"Hi," she said pleasantly to a man coming from that direction.

"Afternoon," he answered.

"Have you seen a couple of kids out this way?"

He smiled. He took off his cap and rubbed his bald head thoughtfully. "Amanda and Aaron? Yep. They're over there watching Mitchell."

"I'm visiting Emma. I'm Elaine Br . . . Webster."

"Pleased to meetcha. I'm Russell Page."

"Oh, Pauline's husband?"

"Same." His smile broadened, showing even white teeth. "You work here, too?"

"Sure do. Me and Polly both. Been here, oh, seven years. We used to work for Laurie Lee when she was in Chicago."

"So did I. I never saw you there."

"Polly worked in her house there. I did a little bit of a lot of things. She's one fine lady."

"I don't really know her. It was a big organization."

"Well, stick around and meet her. She ought to be poppin' in any day now."

"I'd better go find the kids . . . make sure they're not bothering Mitchell. Nice meeting you, Mr. Page."

"Likewise. And call me Russ. Everyone does." He grinned. "Can't never remember to answer to mister."

Elaine found Amanda sitting in the grass outside the pen while Aaron stood close to the wire fence, watching every move that Mitchell made.

"Aren't they magnificent birds?" she asked Aaron.

Mitchell looked up and saw her. He smiled and waved.

"This fellow might just be an animal trainer after all," he told her. "He had a bird eating out of his hand awhile ago."

Aaron swelled with pride.

"Are they bothering you?" she asked.

"Not at all." He nodded in Amanda's direction. "I can't get her to pet them at all, but it didn't take Aaron long to get friendly."

"They're so beautiful. Do you suppose I might be able to paint them?"

He grinned. "They'll pose for free. Throw them a little corn and they'll stand almost still."

"You don't eat them, do you?" She little more than whispered, not wanting tenderhearted Amanda to even hear such a thought.

"Well . . . we mostly sell the eggs, but . . ."

"I see. You know, I didn't even realize that Laurie Lee had a business other than the cosmetic business until your mother mentioned it when I called to ask her if I could come visit."

"Laurie Lee thinks one complements the other."

"Because of the legend?"

"Mother told you, did she? Seems strange, but I guess the Indian lore is good for the cosmetic business. Mother tells me you are planning to go to Los Angeles."

"Your mother seems to think that Laurie Lee might be

able to recommend me for a job out there in her distribution center. Did I tell you I worked for her in Chicago?"

She was surprised that Emma had spoken to her son about her intentions. *Did Emma feel that with the kidnapping of Aaron her presence here might prove embarrassing to her employer if the media found out? Was she so anxious to get them all on their way that she'd even mentioned it to Mitchell?*

"I'd like to go west . . . or north . . . and raise cattle," Mitchell said dreamily.

"Pheasants aren't your thing?"

"Hardly," he said sorrowfully, then gave a rueful laugh.

"You plan to leave?"

He shook his head. "I doubt it. This is a pretty good position and Mother really hates to see me go."

"I see."

"Well, I hope you like Los Angeles if that's where you want to go."

"I'm not sure I have much of a choice."

Aaron came over to stand by her. She dropped an arm around his shoulders.

"I think I'll walk over there to that timber with the kids if that's okay?" She pointed in a westerly direction.

"Sure. There's a nice stream over there. You know, a babbling brook." He smiled. "The kids might enjoy wading."

They set off, Aaron striding boldly ahead, Amanda wading through the tall grasses, clung to her mother's hand. They found the stream and followed its meandering between grassy ledges and rocky protrusions.

"I should have brought my paints," she murmured as Aaron and Amanda dabbled their hands in the clear running water. "If I'm here another day or so, I will."

Chapter Six

On Wednesday morning Elaine, carrying her paint case and collapsible easel with a canvas fastened inside, set out with the children for their second walk to the timber. They crossed the fence and followed the slope of land through tall grasses, and circled around the creek to the spot they admired on a previous walk.

"Did it rain last night?" Aaron examined his shoes that were wet and squishing.

"Dew," she answered, and opened her paint case.

Amanda had already plopped down on the creek bank and was busily removing her own shoes. She toddled down to the water's edge on fat bare feet. Aaron dashed past her and waded boisterously in, making great splashes over both of them. Amanda giggled. Aaron could do no wrong in her eyes.

Elaine let them play while she moved about, searching for the best angle, the best light. She began sketching on a pad, laying out the background, the creek bank, the place where the water trickled over rocks. The trees and bushes on the far side came alive with her effort.

Finally, she called to them. "I want you both to play very quietly now, so I can make a quick sketch."

They sat willing enough. They were in the habit of being the object of her endeavors. After positioning them in her mind and on paper, she started a preliminary painting, mixing different colors to find the proper shadings and values.

She sat lost in thought, thinking of Emma's reaction when she heard the underlying reason why Elaine had brought her stepson with her.

"I still don't understand," Emma had said late yesterday evening when they sat together on the back patio watching the children play.

Elaine felt she owed Emma the whole story and told her of Aaron's fears, how he claimed to have seen Sills kill Roger Reams, and how he felt sure that Sills planned to get rid of him too, to protect himself and Anthony.

"I didn't know Anthony," Emma said, shaking her head at the information. "But I've always known *of* him. I knew he had friends that didn't care much for other's rights. He was investigated several times for fraud and income tax evasion, but I never supposed him to be a . . . a mobster."

"Hard to fathom, isn't it?" Elaine could only wonder why she allowed herself to get involved with him in the first place.

"Surely Aaron is mistaken."

"I'm not so sure."

"He wouldn't see harm come to his only son." Emma protested.

"Wouldn't he? I don't think he cares a whit for him."

Sketching away, and dabbing various colors to her board, Elaine straightened her back and stretched, listening as a bee buzzed over her head in search of nectar. She marveled at the different birds that flew in and out among the leafy branches, and stared upward at white puffy clouds moving lazily in ever-changing shapes across a blue sky.

Contentment stole over her as she made an effort to rationalize what Anthony might or might not do. If only he would consider her flight "good riddance", a remark he'd made about his first wife. Knowing his temperament she doubted he would let them go so easily. She must be alert. Be prepared.

Just because there had been no news on television or in the newspapers didn't mean he wasn't looking for her. Time enough to threaten her with the law. Or with Sills.

Facing her easel, she caught a movement behind the trees that grew across the stream. Her head jerked in that direction. Had it been a breeze that stirred the leafy bushes, or a dog chasing a rabbit? Or had she seen someone darting between the tree trunks?

Her breath caught in her throat. She sat very still, but kept one arm moving in a painting motion without actually putting paint to the canvas. She gazed around, moving only her eyes, straining to determine what she had actually seen, yet being careful to hide the fact that she wasn't painting.

Was someone watching her? Someone who hid behind a tree when her head jerked in that direction? Or was the movement the natural dip and sway of leafy branches catching the breeze?

Still, the notion remained that someone had been there, spying on her. Or the children. She shivered. The children. Worrying about them was more frightening than anything.

The calm she experienced a moment ago was gone. Now the woods didn't seem invitingly quiet, but frightening and full of shadows. Her rationalization of what action Anthony might or might not take was gone, too. Of course he would pursue her. Anthony would never write off the fact that his wife left him, and took not only their daughter, but had also taken his son.

She began folding her easel, her painting enclosed. She tried not to appear in a hurry, but impatiently called, "Let's go," to the children. She helped them with their shoes and they all started the trek back to the house.

It was almost lunch time when they passed by the pheasant pens. Aaron ran over to the fence where a tall, gray-haired man with a decided limp was unloading bags of feed from a truck parked near the pheasant pens. His pale eyes regarded her for a moment before looking away.

"Hi," she called out as Amanda and Aaron stopped to watch in wide-eyed interest.

"Hello," was his indifferent answer, barely glancing up.

"Isn't this a beautiful day?"

"Yep," he said, unenthusiastically.

"The children and I took a walk back by the creek."

"Did Veronica go with you?"

"Why, no," she answered, and thought to herself, *walk with her?* Veronica wouldn't even look at her without glowering.

He turned back to work, a frown of concentration on his face.

Mitchell came around the corner of the building toward them. "Hey, Irving, have you seen Russell?"

"He's supposed to be cleaning those pens out," was Irving's sullen answer.

"He's not there. Hasn't even started on them yet. He was supposed to have them done by now. Well, guess I'll start on them until he gets here."

"Almost lunch time." Irving glanced at his wrist watch.

"It is at that." Mitchell checked his own. "Well, I guess the pens will keep until after lunch." He fell into step beside Elaine who'd called to the children and started with them toward the house.

"Been painting?" was Emma's first question when they entered the family room at the back of the house. "Run and wash up, children. Lunch is almost ready."

As they sat down to eat Mitchell said, "Mother's been telling me that you paint. I know a place you might like to see . . . a perfect spot."

"Where is that?"

"In the same direction you went today . . . only farther. I can show you tomorrow if you like."

"Great. When's the best time? Morning? Evening?"

"Nearer to sunset. I've never stood there at sunset and not thought how it would make a beautiful painting."

"I'd love to see it. Can the children come along?"

"Of course. Say about four tomorrow evening? It's quite a walk, though. I'm not sure about Amanda . . ."

"Maybe Amanda would like to stay with me," Emma suggested, smiling at the little girl. "How about it, Amanda? Shall we go in to Fulton Falls and pick up some things and maybe get an ice cream cone?"

Amanda didn't answer, but seemed to be in deep thought as she concentrated on her dish of tapioca pudding.

"Of course she would," Elaine accepted for her.

"I expect there're a couple of kids who might like to go to the festival at Fulton Falls when it comes." Polly chuckled and picked up the plates from around the table.

"What's a festival?" Aaron's interest piqued at the word.

"Merry-go-rounds, ferris wheels, and all kinds of stuff," Emma answered. "Haven't you ever been to a festival? It lasts all week."

"They've been to circuses and to the zoo," Elaine told her.

"Maybe we can go." Emma's eyes were on the children's faces.

That was all the children could talk about until she tucked them in for the night.

"I think I'll crawl into bed with a book," Elaine told Emma when she went back downstairs.

"There should be something in the library to interest you. I need to go over some household matters with Polly. I'll see you in the morning."

Elaine started down the main hall, snapping on lights and snapping them off again, before she could remember exactly which door opened into the library.

"What are you looking for?" a voice from directly behind her demanded.

Elaine stifled a gasp. One hand flew to her throat. "Veronica," she said with a little laugh, "you startled me."

Veronica made a sound that might have been meant to be a laugh, but there was no humor on her face. "You must be easy to scare. What do you want down here?" The glare from her dark eyes suggested that Elaine was up to no good.

"I want to get a book from the library." Elaine said abruptly, aggravated at Veronica's attitude.

"Then you'd better go in that door over there, the one next to Laurie Lee's office."

"Right. I remember now. Thanks."

An hour later Elaine decided the book she'd chosen should have been left on the shelf. Feeling wide awake she pulled on her robe and went down the back stairs and through the door to the front hallway.

She looked at the first few paragraphs of several books until she heard someone enter Laurie Lee's office. Elaine got very still. She held her breath, waiting. Who would be going into Laurie Lee's office this late? She was doing nothing wrong, but she hoped to avoid another encounter with Veronica if it was her.

Voices came quietly to her ear, but she couldn't decide who was talking. The tone changed. Someone was speaking in disapproving terms.

"I told you I didn't know," came a voice easily recognized as Emma's. "I didn't plan things this way."

"Don't get all ruffled and huffy," came an unknown voice.

"Mother's been disturbed about all this, Laurie Lee. I told you that the minute you heard."

Mitchell's voice. So he was there, too.

"I know. But it seems to me, Emma, that I could have expected a little more discretion from you. I thought you always put my best interests first . . . until now."

"What else could I do once she got here?"

"Knowing what lengths that . . . that man would go to, I'd have thought you would have come up with something."

"I suppose he could cause trouble." Mitchell again. "I hardly knew him. Well, I'm out of here."

When she heard steps coming closer on the other side of the door Elaine darted back into the library. She peeked out in time to see Mitchell heading down the hall.

"I wonder if we could help her find work in Los Angeles . . . get her out of here?" Emma sounded anxious.

Laurie Lee sighed audibly. "I was anxious to get home and now . . . And what about Andrew? Have you heard anything about him at all?"

Andrew? Who was Andrew?

After a moment of silence Laurie Lee, sounding vexed, was demanding, "I really can't understand why you didn't tell me?"

Emma's voice, soothing and calm, was so low that Elaine couldn't make out the words.

Through the crack Elaine watched the shadow of someone pacing back and forth across Laurie Lee's office.

"How can you say such a thing?" Emma was speaking a little louder, a little defiant. "You know I'd never, never do a thing to hurt you."

The voices faded away at Emma's suggestion they make a pot of tea, and the women headed for the kitchen.

Elaine crept back up the stairs to her room. *How could she possibly sleep tonight?* One thing Mitchell was wrong about, Emma didn't always please Laurie Lee.

She lay awake, going over and over past events. If the story concerning Roger Reams was true, maybe that would give her a hold over Anthony. She'd call Lyle Shubin come morning, she decided, to see if Aaron's story could be verified.

She placed the book she'd chosen on a table and bent over the cot where Amanda was sleeping, her arms thrown back over her head. She checked on Aaron who had one palm tucked under a cheek, his long dark lashes fanned out against sunbrowned skin.

"Oh, my darlings," Elaine cried out soundlessly. "I must get us out of here. The sooner the better."

She had never felt so desolate. She had no one to turn to. She'd brought trouble down on Emma without meaning to, and now there was no one else she could count on.

Chapter Seven

The first thing Elaine noticed the next morning were the empty beds where Amanda and Aaron slept. Their pajamas were scattered in heaps about the room. She hadn't even heard them, but she could imagine how they must have been very careful to dress in absolute silence so as not to disturb her, and how they probably crept about, opening and closing the door soundlessly so as not to awaken her.

She pulled on gray slacks and a sleeveless blue blouse and went down the back stairs to the kitchen.

"Good morning, Polly," she said. "Have you seen the children?"

"Heavens, yes. They had breakfast over an hour ago and Emma took them with her to the garden." She folded her hands across her rounded stomach. "What would you like?"

"Nothing, thanks. Coffee, if there's some made."

"Oh, surely you want something." The older woman waited expectantly.

"No, really. I'm afraid I'm upsetting your whole morning as it is." She keenly felt how tenuous her visit was, a guest in the house of a woman who didn't want her nor her children staying on. What would Laurie Lee do? Would she instruct Emma to ship her out at once?

52

"I'm at least going to make you toast," Pauline was saying, bustling off.

Elaine sat down at the table while Pauline moved quickly about the kitchen. The coffee when it came was hot and freshly made, the toast browned to perfection and served with a tray bearing a dish of butter and jars of orange marmalade and honey.

Pauline kept up a running conversation while she ate.

"Laurie Lee got home last night," she said, looking pleased. "Have you met her yet?"

"I used to work for her in Chicago before I was married," Elaine answered. "But no, I haven't seen her since she got in."

How long ago that all seemed now. How odd to think that the people whom she used to consider friends would now be like strangers except for Lyle Shubin, and of course, Emma.

"I've worked here on the farm for Laurie Lee for seven years," Pauline ruminated. "She brought me out here with her when she left Chicago, after her divorce. I never met her husband. I guess he was something else, from what Emma told me. Laurie Lee never mentioned him to me, of course. She's not much for putting anyone down, you know." She nodded her head sagely. "Sometimes I wonder if she's still carrying a torch for him. 'Course I never say nothin'. None of my business. She don't like gossip . . . 'specially . . ." She gave a little chuckle. ". . . 'specially when it's about her."

"Will she be staying here awhile now?" Elaine hoped that something, some pressing business matter might draw her former employer away as quickly as she came.

Elaine had been dreading her first meeting with Laurie Lee and now, knowing how much she wasn't wanted here, she dreaded it even more.

"Well, when I took her breakfast up to her she said she plans to stay here all summer. She looks tired, poor dear."

She clucked her tongue. "She usually comes back at this time of year in time for the Summer Jubilee."

"Summer Jubilee?"

"That's what it used to be called, but now I guess the proper word is 'Pow-Wow.' " Pauline smiled tolerantly. "She invites all of her district managers for a full day of fun and feasting. Keeps me and a couple of girls steppin' though. Russell, too, if he's around." She frowned as she mentioned her husband's name.

Elaine was relieved when she went out of doors to find Laurie Lee nowhere in sight. She wandered across the back yard, circled around the house and stopped in front of the pool sparkling in the sunlight. She couldn't see Emma or the children, but she felt that as long as they were with Emma there was nothing to worry about.

Surmising that they'd gone out to the pheasant pens she went in that direction. Amanda and Aaron never seemed to tire of watching the birds, especially when tiny chicks were hatching.

Before she reached the board fence and the gate that opened onto the outer yard, she noticed Emma walking along, in animated conversation with a tall, dark-haired woman whom Elaine presumed to be Laurie Lee. She wouldn't have known her even though it had only been six years since she worked for her.

This woman wasn't dressed the way Elaine remembered seeing her employer dress years ago when Laurie Lee put in one of her rare appearances where Elaine worked. This woman wore blue jeans and a plaid shirt, whereas Elaine recalled her usually wearing bright-colored clothes that were fragile and floating, more like caftans, sometimes belted, sometimes flowing loose.

As she expected, the children were sitting side by side near the pheasant pens, engrossed in watching Mitchell and Irving throw down bags of feed to Russell who stood with both feet planted firmly on the ground to catch the bags.

"I'll watch them," Mitchell assured her.

She started to cross the yard at a different angle to avoid Laurie Lee, then sighed. It might be better to greet her without the children around should Laurie Lee make it plain that they weren't wanted here.

Emma saw her and threw up a hand in greeting, touching Laurie Lee's arm, drawing her to a halt.

Elaine walked across the yard to meet them, quickening her pace so they wouldn't suspect how she dreaded this moment.

"Laurie Lee, this is my friend, Elaine Webster. Elaine, Laurie Lee." Evidently Emma wanted to keep Laurie Lee in the dark about her married name in the event that Anthony made public what Elaine did. "She used to work for you when she was in Chicago."

Polite exchanges over, Laurie Lee spoke first. "I've met your children," she said in a soft whispery voice, much different than the one raised in anger the night before.

"They were on their best behavior, I hope." Elaine marveled at the beauty and youthfulness of her former employer. She looked no older than she had six years ago.

"Of course they were," Laurie Lee assured her with a smile.

"I've mentioned to Laurie Lee that you are wanting to see about employment in our offices in Los Angeles."

"There are usually openings in almost every department," Laurie Lee commented. She smiled. There were no lines on her face, no wrinkles on her brow, no gray in her hair. *Didn't she ever age?*

No matter what Elaine overheard the night before, Laurie Lee now seemed ready to tolerate her presence temporarily.

"I appreciate that," Elaine said. She felt as though a dark cloud had lifted and while she must make plans to leave, she need not feel she was being rushed out.

Emma and Laurie Lee had lunch on the patio overlooking the pool. White iron chairs with bright striped padded cushions circled the glass-topped table shaded by a colorful umbrella. Elaine and the children ate with Mitchell in the small dining room off the kitchen.

"So you've met the great Laurie Lee." Mitchell came in wearing a clean shirt with the cuffs turned back. He sat down beside Amanda. "I hope you were properly reverent."

Elaine ignored his sarcasm. She was, after all, sitting in Laurie Lee's house, enjoying her hospitality no matter how fleeting, and she wouldn't say one derogatory word about her.

"I've seen her before. Of course I never talked to her. I was just one of her many employees."

"Of course you were," Mitchell said easily. "But my mother is one of her closest friends," he said with exaggerated loftiness.

"They go back a long way, Emma told me." Elaine picked up her salad fork.

"Back to the days of childhood. Mother pretty much raised herself. She and Laurie Lee became friends while they were in grade school. My mother is eternally grateful for all that Laurie Lee did for her." It wasn't difficult to detect a hint of bitterness in his voice.

"Everyone speaks highly of her," Elaine reminded him.

"They're on her payroll," was Mitchell's reply.

"And you?"

He gave her a short, conciliatory salute, smiling in self-depreciation. "I speak highly of her, too."

They ate their salads in silence.

"Are we still on for that jaunt into the woods this afternoon?" He gave Amanda a smile. "And you're going with mother to get an ice cream cone, right, Amanda?"

Amanda stopped eating to look up at him, her elfin face solemn and questioning. Her tongue flicked out to lick the soup from her lips. She nodded slowly, shyly.

"Maybe your mother might be too busy now that Laurie Lee's home," Elaine said doubtfully.

"Surely you've heard that Mother isn't treated as an employee, but a friend." He bent toward her. "Surely you've heard that at least once or twice."

He got up from the table to stand behind Elaine's chair. He leaned over to speak softly in her ear, his tone mocking. "A friend can do anything one chooses."

"Mightn't she choose not to?" Elaine wondered.

"Not my mother." He shook his head. "She told you she'd watch Amanda, she'll watch Amanda." He reached over to give one of the child's pigtails a tug.

Bouncing over rough ground in an old green pickup later in the day, Mitchell's attitude was changed. He was good humored and teasing. He had Aaron laughing all the way.

"So what happened to that surly fellow I lunched with?" she asked lightly.

"I'm sorry about that." He looked at her sheepishly. Laurie Lee brings out the worst in me."

"Well, I'll tell you like Pauline told me early this morning, 'It's none of my business.' "

He laughed, throwing his head back and showing white even teeth. "All the while making it her business, huh? Good old Polly. Her lot in life hasn't been too easy either."

He drove until they topped a final ridge, parking the truck near a fence. They got out. Mitchell lifted out her easel and case from the back of the truck, and helped both her and Aaron across the fence. He carried her things down a hill toward brushy bottom land and timber. She and Aaron trudged along behind.

When they reached the spot that he had in mind she couldn't exclaim over it enough. The setting was far more beautiful than she had even anticipated. A stream meandered steadily along through a grassy field and trickled around crooks and bends, following the lay of the bank as it turned, widening into a little cove that angled sharply around a huge rock that was half in, half out of the water.

Sunlight fell through leafy trees, sending patterns across

the tall grasses, a contrast of dark green along the base of the rocks and the warm olive tones and various shades of reddish-browns in the layers of leaves.

The bank of the rock-lined cove sloped gradually downward. She stepped over a fallen log that rested near the water, the tips of bare branches half-hidden under the rippling surface.

"This is absolutely beautiful, Mitchell," she enthused.

He smiled, pleased.

"There must be several different points of interest right here in this area." She kept moving about, finally opening her easel, and getting out her case. "I'll bet there are a dozen ways of interpreting this scene." She got busy opening tubes of paint, pouring oil and turpentine into different containers, dabbing various hues onto a palette that she held in one hand.

"You needn't feel you should talk to me if it bothers your concentration," he told her.

"It doesn't. Not in the least. I usually talk to the children all the time I'm painting."

"Their chatter doesn't bother you?" He sat down on the rock jutting out over the water, one foot propped against the flat of stone, the other dangling out in front of him.

"I love to listen to them as long as they're enjoying themselves and aren't whining." She smiled, and darted a quick glance at Aaron who smiled back.

"You're never whiny, are you, Aaron?" Mitchell teased.

"Maybe. Sometimes." Aaron admitted, pulling off his shoes and socks.

"My foster parents gave me so much attention while I was growing up," Elaine confided. "I was never told to be quiet, or scolded very much."

"You were an only child."

She nodded. "My parents were killed in a car accident when I was still quite small."

"Then you were a lucky one."

"You're not going to sit there and tell me that you had a deprived childhood?"

"Not deprived." He smiled and watched Aaron splashing about. "Definitely not deprived. Mother went to work for Laurie Lee after my father died when I was ten. We ate, slept and breathed Laurie Lee. Her generosity, how good she was, how helpful, what we owed her. I heard it all. There was nothing Mother wouldn't have done for Laurie Lee . . . even now, for that matter."

"You felt neglected?" she asked incredulously.

He picked up a pebble and tossed it out into the water, the water circling wider and wider around where it fell.

"Listen to me," he said, "a grown man nearing thirty who is crying for his mommy."

"A sad case." She tsked, paying more attention to the outline on the canvas, in getting the colors mixed for the proper shading for depicting light and shadow, than to what he was saying.

"I always had everything," he admitted. "Laurie Lee saw to that. Nothing was too good for Emma's boy. I had the best clothes, as much education as I'd tolerate. Everything handed to me."

"Poor little rich boy."

"Now I'm a farmer . . . of sorts."

"And you're not happy with that?"

"It's not exactly what I want to do. I'd like to have a little more control over my future."

"Excuse me for saying so, but if you're still tied to Mommy's apron strings, isn't it because you want to be?"

"It's not as simple as it sounds."

"Nothing ever is. Easier just to stay on, I suppose."

"I earn my way."

"Then why worry unless you intend to do something about it."

"Like what?"

"Like doing whatever it is you want to do."

He skimmed another pebble across the water. "You're a harpy little critter, aren't you?"

She smiled at him over the top of her easel. "I can be. Anyway, like Polly would say . . . it's none of my business."

"I guess I keep waiting for Mother to cut the strings."

"Shouldn't you do the cutting?"

"You hate to cut away from my mother, don't you?"

"Emma's been very good to me."

"A friend in need . . ."

"Now isn't that original?"

He grinned. "If you're not careful you'll be as grateful to Mother as she is to Laurie Lee."

"And that's a bad thing?"

He shook his head. "You're too sensible for that," he responded.

She didn't answer. She liked being called sensible. Still, she felt the term didn't apply to her. *How could one be called sensible when she'd made off with another person's child?*

Evidently he didn't know about that yet. Emma was really keeping her situation quiet. And isn't that what she wanted?

The fewer who knew the truth, the less likely Anthony would be able to find her.

Chapter Eight

Elaine, absorbed in her painting, finally realized the passing time and gathered up her brushes and tubes of paint. Mitchell, who had gone to sit by the water's edge to talk to Aaron, saw what she was doing and called to her.

"Ready to go?" He strode toward her, his golden hair shining in the sun.

"I think we should get back."

He reached her side. "May I see what you've done?"

"Well . . ." She hesitated for a second. "Yes, of course. I've made several sketches to work on later." She turned the canvas, still wet, around for him to view.

"Me, huh?"

"You made a perfect picture sitting there on that rock. I thought I might give it to your mother."

"That's why you were talking my leg off . . . so I'd sit still and not give you a hard time."

"I'm used to dealing with children," she retorted.

They piled into the truck, the canvases and easel and her painting case in the back, Aaron up front between them. On the drive back, he asked, "Well, was the trip worth it?"

"You were right. It's a perfect place to paint."

He smiled his pleasure at her answer. "I was hoping

you'd think that. I wanted to correct the unfavorable impression I made earlier."

"You made an impression?"

"I'm apologizing for my boorish ways. Quit arguing."

She couldn't help but laugh at him, at the tense way he had of looking at her, as if he was trying to analyze what she was thinking, feeling.

"Apology accepted."

While painting, she had been able to put Laurie Lee's words to Emma out of her mind. Painting could do that for her. And she'd been able, for a little while at least, to put Anthony out of her mind. She was surprised there had been no sign of pursuit, but doubts that he would let her go wouldn't leave. Could he be weighing the consequences of catching up with her against the charges that might be brought against him if Aaron told someone what he'd seen? Anthony wouldn't want the intrusion even if he could prove that Aaron was imagining things.

"You're quiet again," Mitchell said, his eyes on the rough ground they were driving across.

"Just thinking."

He slapped his pockets. "I must have a penny here somewhere," he said.

"Don't bother. They aren't worth a penny. And anyhow, my thoughts are my own."

"Mine, too." He was silent a minute before adding, "but that's about the only thing that's my own. My life belongs to my mother and to Laurie Lee."

"Don't start that again," she warned, smiling, but adamant.

He laughed. "I know. I shouldn't complain. I have a good job even if it's not exactly what I'd like to be doing."

"And that is . . ."

"Didn't I tell you? Raising cattle. Beef cattle."

She nodded. "Oh, yes, you want to play cowboy."

There was no humor in the look he gave her.

"Seriously, I used to work with a friend on his grand-father's ranch every summer. I vowed that someday I'd have my own. Then Mother persuaded me to join Laurie Lee's organization in Chicago. I did for awhile. When I told Mother I was moving on, that I wanted to work out-of-doors, Laurie Lee offered me a job caring for her pheasant farm."

"An offer too good to refuse?"

"I suppose," he admitted. "But they're not cows."

Mitchell parked by the feed shed on their return.

"Can you get everything in okay?"

"Aaron will help me. Thanks again, for taking me."

As she and Aaron passed by the pheasant pens she saw Irving and Russell facing each other in a heated exchange of words. Irving yelled, "Just remember what I told you," then, when he saw that she and Aaron were listening in shocked surprise, he turned and limped away.

She urged Aaron to walk on, wanting to put that sort of unpleasantness out of earshot. Going through the back gate they saw Amanda and Laurie Lee sitting side by side on a glider swing under the shade of a leafy maple.

Laurie Lee was wearing a summer dress of white, a string of bright beads and dangling earrings, and a fragrance that was sweet and familiar, Laurie Lee's *Approachable*.

"Hello," Laurie Lee sang out.

After returning the greeting Elaine gathered Amanda up in her arms, "Did you have an ice cream cone, Mandy?" she asked her daughter.

Amanda nodded, pigtails bobbing.

"Did we ever," Laurie said. "Double dips."

"I had 'nilla and chocolate," Amanda remembered, with a triumphant glance at Aaron.

"Thirty-one flavors and you chose vanilla and chocolate." Elaine tickled her under the chin.

"Emma and I didn't forget you, Aaron," Laurie Lee said

brightly, smiling down at the boy. "We brought back several flavors to please everybody. How about me and you running in and getting you a dish right now to help you cool off?"

His shy smile spread into a wide grin.

"Okay, Laine?" he said, and at Elaine's nod of approval, he scampered after Laurie Lee who was already heading for the back door.

Elaine picked up the case he set down and followed them in. As Laurie Lee proceeded in front of Aaron, he glanced back at her. She saw by his eyes that he was aware of his mistake, and his silent assurance that he would be careful. Elaine was relieved that Laurie Lee hadn't seemed to pick up on the fact that he hadn't called her 'mother.'

Friday dawned cool and cloudy with a soft breeze blowing in from the southwest. Far off in the timber came the call of a rain crow, mournful and forlorn.

Mitchell had asked for permission to take the children to make a short delivery. After they left she stood her easel up in her room, and sat down on a high stool, eager to fill in details on the painting she started yesterday while the impression of light and shadow were still fresh in her mind. She got out her oils.

"Are you going to stay up here painting all morning?" Emma asked later, coming into the room.

"What time is it?" Elaine asked automatically, then, after a quick glance at her clock on the bedside table, she said, "Eleven-thirty. My goodness, I had no idea."

Emma looked at the canvas she was working on.

"Is that Mitch there on a rock?"

"That's your boy."

"Looks like fun," Emma said wistfully.

"Want to try it?" Elaine offered her the brush.

Emma shook her head. "I'm too old," she said.

"Oh, Emma, you're not even fifty," Elaine rebuked.

Emma waved away her words. "I know. But too old to get creative all of a sudden. Besides, I'm too busy."

"Probably hard to fit anything else in . . . what with working for Laurie Lee?"

It was a leading question, but Emma didn't seem aware of its significance.

"Oh, well." She shrugged. "We can't all like to do the same things."

She continued to examine the paintings while Elaine went into the bathroom to wash. When she returned she found that Emma had propped up several others that Elaine had finished and was scrutinizing them carefully.

"I can't speak with any real knowledge of painting, Elaine, but I know what I like and I think you do a superb job. I was thinking . . . there's a man in Fulton Falls who has a gallery. He sells on commission," Emma told her. "You should really see him about selling yours."

"You think so?" Elaine wasn't at all sure that anyone would be willing to do that.

"Tell you what . . . when we go to the festival tomorrow, let's run in there and see him."

"Oh, Emma . . . I don't know . . ." Elaine was doubtful.

"I do." Emma laughed assurance. "Oh, by the way, Laurie Lee wants you and the children to eat lunch with us. I see Mitchell's truck, so they must be back."

"She does? Then I guess I'd better get them in and clean them up if we're to grace Laurie Lee's table," Elaine responded.

Emma looked at her, scrutinizing her much as she had the paintings when she looked at them.

"You're spending too much time with Mitchell," Emma announced, unsmiling.

Elaine stared at her in wonder. "Wh-what do you mean?"

Emma laughed. "You're beginning to sound just like him . . . where Laurie Lee's concerned. Don't be swayed by his opinion. He's biased."

Elaine found the children with Laurie Lee out by the pheasant pens. "I do hope they haven't been making pests of themselves, Miss Randall," she apologized.

"We've been getting acquainted," Laurie Lee answered softly. "And please call me by my name. Everyone does. Even strangers."

Elaine took the children into the house and up to their bathroom to get them cleaned up. *If her former employer was as unconcerned as she appeared to be, had there been another reason for the disagreement that Elaine overheard other than the presence of her and the children?*

Was all not well here in Laurie Lee's paradise?

Over lunch Elaine asked Laurie Lee if she had contacted the Los Angeles office about a possible opening they might have for her.

"I called," Laurie Lee said. "Emma wouldn't let the matter rest until I did." She smiled fondly across the table at her friend.

"What did they say?" Elaine asked anxiously. "Are there any openings?"

Laurie Lee laughed.

"Are you laughing at me?" Elaine felt rebuffed.

"My dear girl," Laurie Lee said in her soft voice. "I don't wish to appear egotistical or smug, but need I remind you that I own the place?" She sipped an icy drink from a crystal goblet with a white frosted design of a pheasant in flight etched in the glass. "Do you think if I told them at the Los Angeles office that I wanted to place someone out there that they would tell me they had no openings?" she appeared amused.

Surprised, and somewhat defiant, Elaine blustered, "I don't mean to sound ungrateful, nor rude, and I do appreciate your help, but that sounds like charity to me . . . having a job created for me just because I'm a good friend of Emma's."

"It never hurts anyone to accept a little charity when

needed, and anyhow, I'd do more than that for Emma."
Laurie Lee's voice was almost fervent.

"I have to admit that going off to work somewhere without anyone knowing where I am . . . totally on my own . . . is frightening. Especially when two children are depending on me for their well being. Having a definite job to go to, would make a world of difference."

Laurie Lee's smile was filled with compassion and understanding.

"Sort of caught between a rock and a hard place, aren't you, Elaine? Well, according to Emma you worked for me in the past, even though I don't remember you at all. But if I hadn't been satisfied with you for some reason, you can be sure I would. And you're not taking charity. Believe me, you'll earn your wages."

"I understand your not remembering me," Elaine said— one hand waving in self-deprecation. "You had so many people in your employ. But I remember you."

"Of course you do." Laurie Lee accepted her words as if they'd been offered in adoration. "Of course you do." She twisted her head to one side as if struck by a sudden thought. "You know, Elaine, it might be a good idea if you were to hang around here until after the Pow-Wow. We have some very helpful insights presented by some of my people who have been with me for years. You could pick up some pointers that could help you make progress with the company."

"But the Pow-Wow is almost a week away, Laurie Lee," Emma's voice raised in objection. "I'm sure that Elaine would rather not wait that long. I think she's anxious to get on her way."

Laurie Lee stared thoughtfully at Emma. "Very well," she said, with what seemed genuine regret. I didn't know you were in such a rush, Elaine. You've been here less than a week. But if you insist, I'll call them again."

"I appreciate it," Elaine said gratefully.

"We'll take the kids to the festival tomorrow for a couple of hours. Eat lunch there. I promised the kids." Emma smiled indulgenly. "Are you going with us, Laurie Lee?"

"Wouldn't miss it," Laurie Lee answered. "I've loved festivals ever since I was a kid."

"Before I leave for Los Angeles I need to get Aaron a few things," Elaine said.

Polly, who came in to pick up the dishes and serve the dessert, spoke up before Emma could respond.

"When I did the laundry I noticed all of Aaron's clothes appear to be new. He must really be growing fast."

Elaine looked at her in dismay. Polly had noticed. Everything was new. *Did nothing escape her keen eyes?*

Laurie Lee and Emma both sat silent, waiting for her answer.

"He's growing like a weed," Elaine conceded firmly, hoping that she sounded nonchalant. Out of the corner of one eye she saw Emma exhale in silent relief.

"If you need to get some things let's you and I and the children run in this afternoon and get that done so you'll be ready to take off. Okay?" Emma smiled, understanding.

"Sounds fine with me."

"And pick out a couple of paintings to take to the gallery. You can tell the manager to contact me when something sells after you've gone to Los Angeles."

"Okay. But that should probably be *'if.'* " Elaine smiled as she left the table. Emma seemed very anxious to have her gone. *Was she trying to spare Laurie Lee further annoyance with Elaine's presence in the household? Or was there another reason?*

Chapter Nine

After lunch, Elaine took the children up to their bathroom to wash them up. They cooperated, eager to be making a trip into Fulton Falls. They ran ahead of Elaine down the back stairs where she drew them to a halt at the sound of voices on the other side of the closed kitchen door.

Russell was backing out of the room into the hall, saying, "Think what you please," and in an injured tone, he added, "You will anyway, no matter what I say."

Elaine couldn't retreat with the children hanging on to her so she cleared her throat to make her presence known. Russell, seeing her, held the door open for them to enter the kitchen where Pauline, face flushed and bright-eyed, was busy taking dishes out of the dishwasher.

She smiled at them, but her smile was a little too set, her eyes, misted with unshed tears, reflected her emotion, and were a bit too bright.

"We're running in to Fulton Falls, Polly," Elaine said kindly, unable to keep from wondering what she and Russell had been arguing about. "Buying Aaron more clothes."

"I know. I need a few things. Veronica has the list. She's out emptying the trash. Will you get it and give it to Emma?"

Elaine found Veronica throwing bags of garbage into a large trash container.

"I'm supposed to pick up a list for Emma," she told the girl.

Veronica reached into the pocket of her jeans and handed her a slip of paper with several items written on it. "I hear you're gonna be leavin' soon," she drawled, her dark eyes dancing.

"I hope to be, yes."

"I'm sure it's for your own good." Veronica's tone of voice sounded more sarcastic than concerned.

"How do you know what's for her own good?" Pauline had come out to stand in the outside doorway. "Why would you possibly care if she goes or stays?"

Veronica shrugged. "None of my business," she said, and whirled around, dragging a trash can behind her. "I just can't figure out what she's doing here anyway?"

"None of your business, or mine." Pauline turned and went back into the kitchen, mumbling, "That's for sure."

"She sounds anxious to see me go," Elaine said.

"She's afraid of competition." Pauline nodded her head sagely.

"Competition? Me? How am I competing?"

"With Mitchell, you know. He took to you right off. I saw that. Veronica's jealous of everyone and everything."

"Nonsense. He's Emma's son, that's all, and Emma's been very kind to me. Anyhow, isn't Veronica married?"

Pauline stifled a snort of derision. "Not that that would stop her. She gives Irving fits. Tells him if he can't make more money she'll find someone who does . . . someone who can take her to Florida. It really bugs her that Irving is Laurie Lee's relative and they have to work for her like everyone."

Elaine gave a short laugh. "Well, she needn't worry about me. I'm not the slightest bit interested in Mitchell."

Before hurrying off to join Emma who was ready and waiting, she added emphatically, "Not that way."

Fulton Falls was a small town that suited the residents who liked friendly neighborliness. A place where even strangers became familiar. Most of the businesses were located along the court house square. The block building stood in the center of a green lawn, complete with a statue of the founding father looking with pride out over the town. Down the street she noticed a sign advertising the art gallery.

Emma found a parking space in front of the pharmacy where photos of fountain drinks adorned the glass windows. The sight drew both children to a standstill to eye them yearningly.

"We'll go in here at Bricker's for the clothing first and then have sodas when we are done," Emma promised, locking Elaine's painting in the trunk of her cream-colored Mercury.

The interior of Bricker's was cool. A striped awning hung over the front windows shading the interior from the sun. Elaine followed Emma into the store and up a half flight of stairs to the children's department.

Elaine, not used to shopping for Aaron, found it more time-consuming than she expected, but finally settled on a pair of dress pants, a shirt, and some shorts for play. Aaron, who could care less about what he wore, was bored.

"I want a dress," Amanda said peevishly, pulling at a dress hanging from a rack of dainty ruffled frocks.

"You don't need dresses, Mandy," Elaine told her firmly. Seeing her disappointment she relented a little. "Perhaps a playsuit or a new top?"

"I want to look at some things I noticed down on the first floor," Emma said. "Why don't I go on down and look while you help Amanda? Here . . ." She held out her arms.

"Let me take this stuff you've already got picked out for Aaron. You can look easier without your arms full."

"We won't be long," Elaine told her.

Amanda was being fussy. She didn't like trying on clothes, but Elaine had no intention of buying unless she did.

"I want to go down with Emma." Aaron soon got restless and bored. "She's right down there," he pointed. Elaine looked out over the wood banister to the floor below where Emma was standing with her back to them.

"All right," Elaine consented. "Maybe Mandy will settle down and try these things on if you aren't around distracting her."

Finally, the decision made for one sun dress, a pair of shorts and a matching top, she took the articles with her and started down the stairs, holding Amanda by the hand. They moved slowly down behind two elderly ladies who were more interested in talking to each other than they were in making their way down the steps.

Suddenly, she stiffened in shock.

"Mommy, you're squeezing my hand," Amanda whimpered.

A chill of fear had erupted in the pit of Elaine's stomach and her heart fluttered in sick dread. Over at the opposite end of the same rack that was holding Emma's attention was the one person she hated most to see other than Anthony.

Martin Sills.

Down below as if in a slow motion panorama Elaine saw Aaron walking carelessly along between other racks of clothes, headed with unconcern toward the spot where Emma stood. Standing at the end of the rack, unnoticed as yet by Emma, was Sills, an evil smirk simpering across his face as he waited like a cat might wait for an unsuspecting mouse to walk into his clutches.

Elaine watched helplessly. Should she try to attract

Aaron's attention? But if she did, might she also attract Sills who was so obviously enjoying his little game?

Grabbing Amanda up under one arm, Elaine pushed her way past the two ladies and dashed madly down the stairs.

One of the women grabbed hold of the rail and gasped, "Did you ever . . . ?"

Elaine never stopped to apologize, but darted as fast and as quietly as she could across the crowded floor, hoping to catch Aaron before he could start up the next aisle which would bring him face to face with Martin Sills.

She came up on the opposite side of the rack, and without thinking or caring how her action might be misconstrued by those watching, she reached between the folds of hanging clothing and grabbed Aaron by the collar of his shirt, dragging him through. The clothes swayed and a few fell to the floor.

Aaron's mouth flew open until he saw that it was Elaine who held him. Before he could make a sound Elaine clapped her free hand around his mouth to stop him from saying anything, and pulled him off in the opposite direction.

Two young women shoppers standing close by, glared at her, frowning their disapproval. Amanda giggled from her awkward position under Elaine's arm. She thought this must be some kind of game. Elaine bent over and whispered the word, "Sills," in Aaron's ear, causing him to press trustingly close to her side, stilling the women's suspicions.

She rushed him toward the store exit, dropping the clothing she'd chosen for Amanda on the checkout counter as she passed by.

Chapter Ten

Elaine never hesitated in her headlong flight out of Bricker's into the bright sunlight, gripping one of Aaron's hands and holding Amanda in her arms. Breathing heavily, she headed directly to Emma's car parked in front of the pharmacy, but before she could take two steps more in that direction, she stopped, her heart lurching in panic.

Parked a few cars behind Emma's was a limousine she recognized at once, and leaning on the hood of the limo with his back to her, was Anthony.

He stood, one arm draped on the polished metal hood and looked nonchalantly around. He hadn't noticed her yet. His attention seemed to be focused on a group of children running about the courtyard.

Elaine gasped and drew the children to an abrupt halt. She couldn't go to Emma's car with Anthony so near. He would be certain to notice her if she took one more step in that direction.

She yanked both childen up the entrance and through the doorway into the ancient-looking pharmacy next to Bricker's. Cool air engulfed her as she led them down an aisle in the middle of the store, hoping to find some spot to hide. If Anthony decided to come in she wanted to be out of sight.

"May I help you?" a pleasant voice inquired. A middle-aged woman approached her with a friendly smile.

"Oh, please," Elaine began, drawing in a long and shaky breath. "I'm from out of town and I need to make a phone call to have someone come pick us up."

"Did you come in on the bus?" The woman made no move to direct her to a telephone.

Elaine tried to remain calm, composed and unruffled, but when she heard the bell tinkle above the door that opened onto the street, she jerked nervously around, her heart pounding, to see who was entering.

Her eyes closed in relief when she saw that the person who entered was not Anthony, but an elderly lady with a shopping bag over one arm.

"Good morning, Tillie," the clerk said to the newcomer. "We got in that fragrance you've been wanting."

"Please." Elaine interrupted. "May I use your phone?"

"Local call?" The woman was unhurried.

Assured that it was, the clerk waved a hand toward the back of the store near the pharmacy section, then turned back to give her customer her full attention.

Veronica answered the phone, but when Elaine requested that someone come pick up her and the children she replied flippantly, "Something wrong with Emma's car?"

"I'll explain later. Can you come?"

"To Fulton Falls? Hardly. Old Pollyanna has laid out enough work to keep me busy for a week. What did you say happened?"

"I said we need a ride home. We'll be in the alley behind Watkin's Pharmacy."

"Russ can probably come," she said, then added slyly, "or did you want me to send Mitchell? But I expect old Mitchell is pretty busy this time of day."

"Emma says to tell Mitchell to come right away," Elaine lied. "Come down the alley behind the pharmacy."

"Okay. Okay. I'll tell him." The receiver at the other end banged down.

Looking out the window at the front of the store Elaine could see Anthony, dark brows almost a straight line across his forehead, hat off, his face perspiring. She saw him glance almost longingly toward the advertising fastened to the windows and could guess that he was debating stepping inside for a cold drink.

Even as she was surmising what he intended to do, he took a step in the direction of the store.

Hanging onto Aaron's arm, and gathering up Amanda she hurried past the pharmacy counter and into the back part of the store just as the bell tinkled again, announcing a new arrival. She didn't look to see if it was Anthony, but kept her face turned in the opposite direction.

The pharmacist followed her into the back room.

"Lady," he said uncertainly, "what are you looking for?"

"The back door. Please."

There must have been something in her voice that caused him to listen to that one word of appeal. He shrugged his white-jacketed shoulders and escorted her around a maze of shelves and boxes to a door that opened onto the alley.

"Please," she said in little more than a whisper as he closed the door behind her. "Please don't tell anyone that you've seen us."

Walking out onto the rock surfaced alley, she tried to decide what to do next. Seeing no one in either direction, she let Amanda slide out of her aching arms to stand down beside her.

How long would it take Mitchell . . . or someone . . . to reach Fulton Falls? A half hour? Or longer? She crept down the length of the alley, watching warily in all directions and keeping the children close. She wondered how Emma managed when she ran into Sills? Elaine could only hope that she saw him in time to be prepared, and realize that Elaine must have seen him and quickly exited the store.

"Where we goin'?" Amanda demanded.

Before Elaine could answer or head for the other end of the alley, a small white poodle dashed out from behind a bushy border along someone's yard. The poodle yapped sharply, first at one of them and then at another. Amanda let out a piercing shriek and tried to climb up in Elaine's arms. Aaron, greatly delighted, making just as much noise as Amanda, chased after the dog. The poodle, barking constantly, kept beyond his reach.

Elaine braced herself for an instant realiziation. The noise from the barking dog and the screaming children was bound to attract someone's attention if they were within hearing distance. If Sills had just then been walking by to join Anthony, he would have been sure to hear the disturbance and come to investigate. The thought of Sills and his silky smile made her shudder. He would have to bodily tear them away from her before she would let them go with him.

She knew they couldn't just continue to stand there in the middle of the alley without being discovered. Quieting Amanda as best she could, Elaine carried her farther down the alley. Aaron followed. The poodle quit barking as soon as they left the area that he evidently considered his, and disappeared behind the bushes.

The rear entry of an ice cream store beckoned. She was hot and thirsty and knew the children must be, too. The thought of sitting in a booth sipping tall cool sodas was very tempting, but she rejected the idea almost at once. Might not Sills be tempted by the same desire? And might he reason that the ice cream store would be a likely spot for her to take the children?

If he walked by the end of the alley, he would have a clear, unobstructed view of of them standing there, for there was nothing to block his vision in the empty alleyway.

She had to get the children out of sight, yet be close enough to spot Mitchell or whoever arrived to get them. She stayed away from the area claimed by the poodle to walk a few feet farther where she could see an opening in the same hedge.

There was no sound of a dog, for which she was extremely grateful. On the other side of the hedge stood a wood-slatted screen designed to camouflage several garbage cans. She drew the children through the hedge and behind the screen. The slats only partially hid them, still, somehow she felt more secure there than out in the open.

No sooner had she stood Amanda down on her feet when a door banged and a little girl, perhaps ten years of age, came out of the house toward their place of concealment.

The little girl skipped along, dragging a black plastic bag behind her. She came around the corner of the screen, saw them standing there staring at her, and came to a sudden stop. For a few moments no one moved. Then Elaine smiled reassuringly and quietly said, "Hello."

The little girl never answered and Elaine could see a question taking shape in her mind, but her eyes never left off staring at them.

"We're waiting for a friend," Elaine explained casually, as if it were perfectly normal to use someone's garbage screen as a waiting place.

The little girl took one step backward, still clinging to the plastic bag, eyes watching them warily, but not making a sound.

"Seems like a good place," Elaine continued calmly, "to get out of the heat."

She realized as soon as the words were out of her mouth that the sun was bearing down on them from the open top and through the slatted sides—offering no relief at all. *And with a shade tree in the corner of the yard near the alley, and an ice cream parlor located but a few feet farther on, who would be gullible enough to accept her excuse?*

"Mama," the little girl called out, and took another step backward. A loose end of the garbage bag caught on a rough edge of a stepping stone. She never noticed, but continued dragging it as she went back up the steps to the rear door of the house.

"Mama," the child hollered louder, unaware that her bag was split open and was strewing garbage up the steps.

A woman appeared in the doorway.

"Martha Sue," the woman scolded in dismay. "What on earth are you doing? Can't you be more careful? I send you to do the simplest chore . . ."

"But, Mama . . ." the child protested.

"Get another bag," her mother told her. "And pick up that mess. Now." The screen door banged as the woman went back inside the house.

The child had no choice. With a new bag in one hand she picked up the papers and bottles and other junk that had tumbled out and carried the new bag slowly toward Elaine's hiding place.

Elaine smiled reassurance as the girl removed a can lid and stuffed the bag inside the container.

"Mama," the girl called, backing away.

Amanda smiled at her, too, winsome and appealing.

"Let's go, children," Elaine said gently, wanting to be gone before the child's mother saw them and became alarmed.

Come on, Mitchell, Elaine thought almost desperately. She led the children through the hedge into the alley, praying for Mitchell to hurry. As if in answer to her prayer she saw his pickup coming toward them.

They got in. She sighed with relief as the cool air circulated around them through the vents on the dashboard.

"Oh, that air feels good," she said, feeling safe again. "Thank you for coming so quick."

"What's wrong?" Mitchell drove on down the alley. "Where's Mother?"

"She'll be along in her own car. She's okay. Can I explain after we get back to Laurie Lee's?" She cast a telling glance at the children.

"Of course." He headed out of town without another word.

"Emma promised me a soda," Amanda whined.

"Sh-h-h." Elaine gave her a comforting hug.

Emma returned before lunch, but it wasn't until Laurie Lee went up to her room that Elaine got a chance to ask questions, and to clarify her own actions.

"I saw Martin Sills from the upstairs of Bricker's," Elaine explained, and proceeded to tell the rest of her story. As she finished, she said, "Did Martin say anything to you?"

"Oh, yes. You could have knocked me over with a feather when I got to the end of the rack and saw him standing there with that gloating smile on his face. He tried to get me to admit that you were staying with me, which I denied, of course. I told him I hadn't seen you, so he wanted to know why I was buying little boy clothing; the ones I carried for you were still draped over my arm. I told him they were for a grandson. I had to shop around for hours it seemed like, before he quit following me. And all the while I was worried sick about you and the kids. By the way, I took your painting into the art gallery before I left town."

"What's to keep him . . . or Anthony . . . from coming here and demanding the children?"

"I doubt he'll do that. Anything he does will probably be underhanded. He won't want a lot of publicity."

"I hope you're right. I guess the sooner I go to Los Angeles, the better."

"I figured that's how you'd feel." Emma stood up. "Laurie Lee wants to go over some suggestions for this year's Pow-Wow. We'll talk again later." She patted Elaine on the shoulder.

When she and the children walked out to the pheasant pens before the evening meal, Mitchell came over to where they stood. Looking tan and fit, his shirt collar open, he smiled and said, "Well, the kids are too interested in the pheasants to listen to us . . . do I hear what's going on, or am I to be kept in the dark?"

She moved closer to him and dropped her voice. A short distance away the children were discussing which pheasant was the prettiest.

"I thought your mother might have told you," she answered.

"All Mother would say was that your husband is giving you trouble. Excuse me for presuming, but there seems to be more to it than that."

She had intended to continue with the entire lie, but something about Mitchell's eyes when they looked into hers, something warm and caring made her confess more of the truth than she intended.

"I took the children without Anthony's consent," she admitted, but she didn't mention that Aaron was not her son. "That's why I'm anxious to go to Los Angeles."

"And why Mother is eager for you to go. I wondered about that. Mother's been as nervous as a cat. Does Laurie Lee know this?"

"I don't believe so."

He whistled. "Laurie Lee's death on bad publicity. When do you think you'll be leaving?"

"As soon a I can. Evidently Anthony and Sills figured I'd come here. I really think I shouldn't take the kids to the festival. I know your mother wants us to go, but I'm more afraid than ever now."

But later that evening when Elaine suggested they stay close to the farm until time for her to leave, Emma protested. "I told those children we were going to the festival, and we're going," she said firmly.

"Is there a problem?" Laurie Lee came into the room.

"No. No problem," Emma said instantly.

"Good. Oh, Emma, I left that list for mailing reminders to my new managers on my desk. Can you get started on them?"

"Sure." Emma always seemed agreeable. "Right away."

"Can I do something to help?" Elaine offered, noticing how tired Emma looked.

"You can help stuff envelopes and check current addresses."

In Laurie Lee's office, Emma pawed about on the desk while Elaine stood ready to do what she could.

"She did say she left the list here, didn't she?" Emma said. "Look over there on that side table, will you, Elaine? I can't figure out what she did with it." Emma was going through a sheaf of papers.

Elaine examined some of the papers scattered on the table that stood next to a wall.

"I don't see anything that looks like a list."

"Nor here either." Emma sighed. "Look in those drawers, then, will you? She might have put it in there and forgotten that she did."

There were two drawers to the table. Elaine opened first one, then the other, but she found nothing in either that looked like a list. Just as she closed the second drawer, her attention was caught by a newspaper clipping, a photo with the caption cut at an angle so only part of it was readable.

Even if she hadn't caught the name Bradford, she would have recognized the house at once, a close-up of the back yard of the house that had been, if not a home, the place where she resided for four years.

What was a photo of Anthony's house doing here in a drawer at Laurie Lee's? The print was fuzzy, and she couldn't make out who all was standing in a little group together. One of them, a man, looked an awful lot like a younger Anthony might have looked.

She showed it to Emma. "This seems to be a newspaper

clipping showing a picture of Anthony's house in Chicago."

"So that's where I left it," Emma said without hesitation. She took it from Elaine, and giving it only the barest glance, wadded it up and threw it in the wastebasket.

"I wasn't aware that you were on friendly enough terms with my husband to want a picture from a newspaper."

"He was one of Laurie Lee's investors back then. I think he's sold his shares now. Anyhow, it's not important anymore. I found the list. Shall we get to work?"

All afternoon while they worked Elaine couldn't quit thinking about the newspaper clipping. When Emma left the room to consult Laurie Lee about someone's name, Elaine took the clipping from the wastebasket and shoved it into a pocket of her slacks.

Elaine slept in late the next morning. She and Emma had worked until after midnight preparing the reminders to Laurie Lee's managers. She carried her coffee out to the patio to drink, but she had taken only a few sips when Polly called from the back door.

"You've got a telephone call, Elaine."

Wondering who on earth could be calling her, Elaine reentered the kitchen.

"Mrs. Webster? This is Sam from the art gallery. I sold one of your paintings yesterday afternoon."

Elaine couldn't believe what she was hearing.

"Which one?" she asked.

"The one of your children playing with a garden hose. The man snapped it right up."

A tremor of alarm rippled through Elaine's body.

"Who bought it?" She tried to sound casual, but she gripped the telephone tighter in her hand.

"Let me see . . . Oh, yes, an Anthony Bradford."

Why would Anthony buy one of her paintings? Just so she would know he was around? To put fear in her?

One thing she was certain of, he didn't buy it because

of love for art, especially her art. He could afford paintings by the masters if he chose.

She went to Emma with her fears.

Emma took one look at her face and said, "What's wrong?"

Elaine wrinkled her nose ruefully.

"Do you want the good news first, or the bad news?"

"What?"

"The art gallery called and said they'd sold one of my paintings."

"That is good news." Emma beamed her congratulations. "What's the bad news?"

"Anthony was the one that bought it. He must have gone in there and recognized the children in the painting. I think he did it as a warning to me."

"Oh, no."

"He might have asked the owner of the gallery for my address," she added fearfully.

"Oh, Elaine, he'd be able to get your address in a dozen different ways."

"You're probably right." Elaine was trembling. "But I can just see him distracting the man while Sills snooped into his sales book."

"What can I do?"

Elaine spread her hands in a hopeless gesture.

"It's like we're sitting ducks . . . the kids and I. He might creep in here some night and just snatch them."

"Oh, I doubt that. There are too many people sleeping in this house. Snatching someone wouldn't be all that easy."

"I wish Laurie Lee would hurry with that job reference, even though I hate to think about going off to Los Angeles all by myself," Elaine admitted, then added with a deep sigh, "but I hate worse just sitting here thinking Anthony could grab Amanda or Aaron at any time."

Emma dropped a comforting arm around her shoulders. "I know. I'll see what can be done right away."

"I'm really frightened about taking the kids to the festival. I'm sure Anthony or Sills will be watching for us. Don't you think we should call off going?"

"I think you'll be safe enough, Elaine. Everyone's going, Mitchell, Irving and Veronica, and even Polly and Russell. And of course, Laurie Lee. I really think you'll all be in good hands."

Elaine said nothing more, but she worried. Something told her not to go. But the others, not sensing the same fear that she felt, were insistent.

Chapter Eleven

The next morning, Elaine, still upset over what happened at Brickers, put in a call to Lyle Shubin the moment she got downstairs. No one was in the kitchen. She supposed that everyone was doing their own thing in preparation of the jaunt into town for the festival.

Greetings over, Lyle demanded, "Where are you?"

She hesitated a moment before answering. *But what harm could it do?* she reasoned. She was leaving for Los Angeles right away.

"I'm visiting Emma," she said.

"She still works for Laurie Lee, doesn't she?"

"Yes. Yes, she does." She didn't want to linger on details. "I want to ask a favor, Lyle. Would you check around and see if a man by the name of Roger Reams is missing or has been found dead recently?"

"Roger Reams? Why on earth would you want to . . . he's a regular hoodlum, Elaine."

"I'd rather not say why I want to know, Lyle. Please, just check for me, subtly, of course. Don't tell anyone . . . not anyone, Lyle, that I'm the one wanting to know."

"What's going on? You say you're with Emma? I remember her. She was Laurie Lee's Girl Friday."

"Right." She didn't tell him that Emma was still very close . . . in fact, living right in Laurie Lee's house.

She had been surprised when Laurie Lee said she was intending to go to the festival. Elaine hadn't supposed that would be something she would do for pleasure.

She had refrained from questioning Emma about Laurie Lee's disapproval of her and the children staying there after Emma had made it clear she could ask guests anytime she chose. *What was it that caused Laurie Lee such anguish, and such anger? Why did she object to Elaine so strenuously?* She hoped to find out before leaving for Los Angeles. She had no intention of staying for the Pow-Wow.

Putting Aaron and Amanda at the kitchen table to eat their cereal, she went in search of Emma. Finding her room empty she retraced her steps down the stairs and out onto the back patio where Emma was waiting patiently for the others to get ready to go. Dark circles ringed her eyes. She looked worried and tired.

"Are you all right, Emma?" she voiced her concern.

"Oh, yes." Emma gave her a wan smile.

"I wanted to ask you about Laurie Lee's argument with you the night she came home. I was in the library and heard you."

Emma showed no surprise. "I'm sorry we woke you."

"Laurie Lee seemed to be blaming you for something," Elaine persisted. "Was it something to do with me?"

"Don't be paranoid, Elaine," Emma said reproachfully. "Must everything be about you?"

"I didn't suppose Laurie Lee ever got upset with you, or you with her." Elaine didn't feel satisfied with Emma's answer, or lack thereof.

Emma frowned. "Laurie Lee had every right to be upset with me. I could never be angry with her. When we were girls she saved me from a life of poverty. Her foster father had plenty of money and gave her every advantage . . . tried to satisfy her every whim." Emma's mouth twisted in a self-indulgent smile. "One of her whims was me."

"I thought maybe she'd found out about Aaron?"

"Aaron?" She appeared startled.

"That I'd taken him without consent. You said she's terrified of bad publicity. If the newspapers found out they'd have a field day."

"Tell me, Elaine . . ." Emma's voice sank to a whisper. "Aren't you sorry you brought him? Got yourself in such a mess? Wouldn't it be better if you just called his father to come get him?"

"Oh, no." Elaine was horrified. "I could never do that to Aaron. Anthony wouldn't pat me on the back for telling him. He'd have to get even. He'd retaliate by trying to take Amanda from me."

"You could just talk to him . . . or let me talk to him . . ."

Elaine emphatically shook her head. "No, no, no." If she dared tell Emma about Roger Reams, Emma might realize why she was so adamant in her determination to keep their whereabouts secret from her husband.

Emma got up. "I think I'll see if everyone's ready to go."

"Are you sure you feel up to going, Emma?"

"Of course. The kids have been looking forward to it."

Elaine wasn't. Something in her subconscious mind whispered that going to Fulton Falls was not only foolish, but quite possibly dangerous.

"I'm sort of afraid . . . for the children," she confided.

"I can understand that," Emma soothed. "But Fulton Falls is a fair-sized town and there'll be a huge crowd there today, being Sunday. So even if Sills is still around, the family will be with you and the children to protect you all the the time. Everyone's going in the van except Irving and Veronica. They're driving their own car."

"I was surprised when Laurie Lee said she was going."

"She never does," Emma remarked, and frowned thoughtfully.

Mitchell drove the van. The seven adults and the two children rode together. Pauline declined their repeated invitation.

"I'm gonna sit here and just relax," she insisted.

The town of Fulton Falls swarmed with people. Rides filled Main Street. Music jangled from the carousel. The aroma of freshly-popped corn filled the air.

They all stayed in a group at first. Veronica twisted about, seeming to believe she was being provocative, as she slyly invited Mitchell to ride with her on the Tunnel of Love.

"Thanks, but that's not for me," Mitchell declined.

"Act your age, Veronica," Irving growled, giving his wife a frosty look.

Veronica hurried to catch Emma. "Wouldn't hurt your son to loosen up a bit," she said. "He's a real stick in the mud."

Emma only glared at her, but Laurie Lee said, "Now, Veronica," in her soothing voice, and pointed out something spectacular that Aaron and Amanda should look at.

Eventually the group split up to pursue individual choices of entertainment. Before Laurie Lee left with someone she knew, she settled the question of where to meet for lunch.

"Elaine's too polite to say, but I know a boy who's been talking about eating at the Circle Inn."

So it was decided.

Amanda grew tired long before Aaron. Elaine sank down on a park bench under a shade tree with Amanda beside her, her head on her mother's lap. Emma was taking Aaron to see a skateboard race. "See you at one at the Circle Inn," she told Elaine.

"Upstairs or down?" Elaine wondered.

"Laurie Lee said upstairs," Emma reminded her. "That's where Aaron wanted to go. Remember? Coming, Mitch?"

"I think I'll stay here and keep Elaine company," he said, dropping down on the bench beside her, and stretching his long legs out in front of him. "Having fun?" he asked, regarding her curiously.

"It's nice to watch the kids have fun."

"You're just a kid yourself." He smiled.

"I don't feel like a kid."

"That's because you worry too much. How old are you, twenty-five?"

"Twenty-nine. And you?"

"I'm old. Thirty-four. You're quite a mother, you know."

"For some reason, that doesn't sound like you're complimenting me. What are you thinking?"

"Simple mathematics. If you're twenty-nine, and Aaron's ten, and if you were married a year before you had him. . . . I think I heard you mention that you went to college for two years, and you worked for Laurie Lee awhile before you got married . . . let's see . . . you must have been about fourteen when you graduated from high school." He smiled, but there was a question in his eyes.

She felt her face flush. She wasn't used to lying. How stupid of her, and how obvious her lie would have been if she'd given it any thought. But she hadn't. And that was always her trouble.

She opened her mouth to answer, but no words came.

"Gotcha." One eyebrow shot up.

"Not impossible," she retorted.

"Not probable. Why are you playing games?" A smile touched his lips, but his eyes appraised her coolly.

"I'm not playing games," she countered, angry, but mostly directing the anger toward herself.

"Sounds like Russian Roulette to me. Kind of a dangerous game to play."

"I'm really not that concerned about what you think."

He watched her from under lowered lids. "My question is," he said steadily, "does my mother know?" When she didn't answer immediately, he added, "Or are you lying to her, too?"

"Why don't you ask her?"

"I have. She never answers. I know something is really wrong, but I just don't know what."

She stood up and drew a sleepy Amanda to her feet. She seethed with unfocused rage . . . at herself . . . at Anthony . . . at Mitchell. She left him sitting there and headed down a street in the general direction of the Circle Inn.

There was time to spare before one o'clock so she urged Amanda to take a short walk to the duck pond. The purchase of a bag of crumbs kept the child interested as she threw out the crumbs slowly and in careful consideration for each duck.

By the time Amanda could be coaxed to leave the pond, they were a few minutes late. A large crowd had gathered outside the entrance to the restaurant.

"My goodness, Mandy, do you suppose all these people are wanting to eat at the same place?" She stood at what she supposed was the end of a line, keeping a firm grip on Amanda's hand until the crowd closed in.

"I can't see," Amanda wailed.

She picked Amanda up in her arms. From the murmuring she soon deduced that something was wrong. "What is it?" she asked anxiously of first one person and then another. No one seemed able to answer. An accident, someone said, but no one seemed able to offer an explanation of what kind.

A disturbing thought lurked in her mind.

Where was Aaron? Surely Emma would keep him with her at all times. Elaine heaped self-incriminations on her own head. *Why had she let him go off without her? Why had she been so negligent when Aaron trusted her judgment to keep him safe?*

The crowd suddenly parted, sounds of sympathy rippling down the line, then quieting again as an emergency crew passed through their midst and placed a stretcher in a waiting ambulance. She couldn't see who was on the stretcher for the body, face and all, was completely covered.

An icy knot formed in the pit of her stomach. Her knees threatened to buckle with the fear that arose, filling her throat until she could barely breathe. Still holding Amanda she took a step back as the ambulance moved away from the curb.

She pressed forward toward the entrance to the Inn, assuring herself that the body on the stretcher couldn't have been Aaron. Whoever was covered with that cloth was surely much larger than a child.

A familiar voice called her name.

"Elaine." It was Mitchell. Relief at seeing him was so great that she felt dizzy.

"Who was it? What happened?" she demanded, anxious and worried. "Aaron. Is he okay?"

"Mother said that someone fell from the second level down through to the basement. The Cellar, I believe it's called."

"Did you see it happen? Who was it?"

"No, I never saw it, but Mother seemed to think that you might know of him . . . Martin Sills, she said. The police seem to think that he jumped. They'll investigate, of course."

Thinking back to her first trip to the Circle Inn, she recalled how her stomach flip-flopped when she stood on that upper level and looked down.

"Martin Sills would never jump," she said with certainty. Suicide wasn't the nature of a person who cared little about anyone but himself, someone who would not suffer from a bad conscience.

"The police are taking names and addresses of everyone who was up there at that time. Mother and Laurie Lee will

be along shortly. I kind of crashed the line to reach you so
you wouldn't try to go up." He nodded toward an officer
in the doorway. "I guess you wouldn't have got by those
guys anyway." He smiled down at Amanda who was snug-
gling one of her hands into his. "Here they come now," he
said, spotting Emma and Laurie Lee, hurrying Aaron along
the walk leading out from the Inn. A few steps behind them
was Veronica who, for once, wasn't being brazen, but
looked shaken and ill.

"Did you see what happened?" Elaine asked Emma when
she joined them on the walk still jammed with the curious
onlookers.

"No, thank God," Emma answered. "I had gone into the
restaurant to tell the hostess to save us a large table for
lunch. When I came out there was all this commotion."

"I'm shaking," a pale Laurie Lee confessed, her voice
husky. She lay one hand on Mitchell's arm as if to steady
herself.

"Did you see it happen?" Mitchell asked solicitously,
holding onto her.

She shook her head. "I heard," she said, then closed her
eyes as if blocking out some image in her mind.

Irving hurried from the sidelines to join them. His face
was flushed, and he was glaring at his wife.

"Where were you, Veronica?" he demanded roughly,
grabbing her by the shoulder.

"What do you mean, where was I?" she snapped. "I was
where I was supposed to be, waiting for you in front of the
art gallery."

"I've been waiting there," he protested indignantly, darting accusing eyes at Mitchell. "You were probably riding
the ferris wheel with someone . . . acting like a stupid teenager."

"Watch your face, Irving," Mitchell growled. His mother
reached out and placed a warning hand on his arm which
he promptly shook off.

"I guess you haven't heard about the suicide?" Veronica was eager to share bad news.

Irving's attention changed at once. "Suicide? What suicide?" He blinked owlishly.

"Someone . . . someone that I think Elaine here knows . . . jumped down into The Cellar from the second floor."

"His name was Martin Sills," Emma, her eyes on Elaine, seemed to be sending a message, a warning for her to be careful of how she answered.

"Yes," Elaine little more than whispered. "I did know him slightly. He was a business acquaintance of my husband's."

"The police will probably want to talk to you." Veronica seemed to get satisfaction out of that revelation. She looked around as if she would notify a policeman if she could get to one.

Irving grabbed her by the arm and led her away.

"I never even got into the Inn," Elaine told Mitchell. "Amanda and I were feeding the ducks."

Chapter Twelve

The day was ruined. Not because anyone felt grief, but because of the unexpected and unusual death of another human being. For some reason, a saying came to Elaine: *No man is an island.* Not even Sills. She supposed he must have a family somewhere. A mother? Father? Siblings?

No one spoke much on the way home, partly out of deference to the children's presence, and partly because of the subdued atmosphere.

Even the children were quieter than usual. She could understand Aaron's silence. After all, he had known Martin Sills. Even though he mistrusted him, even feared him, his sudden death had a sobering effect.

When they got back to the farm, she took the time to sit with him at the table for milk and cookies.

"Sometimes things just happen for no reason," she told him, not mentioning that she had already discounted in her own mind that Martin would deliberately jump to his death.

"I don't think it just happened, Laine," he told her, his voice little more than a whisper. His eyes on hers were round and unblinking.

"What do you mean?" She bent closer.

He looked around the family dining room, making certain they were alone. "Father was there. I saw him."

In spite of the warm day, she shivered. "What do you mean? What are you suggesting?"

"Father followed Emma and me when we got off the ferris wheel. I told Emma I saw him, but she thought I was just 'magining things. She said it must have been someone who looked like Father. But I was scared, so we sneaked ahead of the others into the restaurant. When we got up on the second level, she said she saw him, too . . . that he was coming, up the stairs to where we were, so she had me hide behind some folding doors."

Elaine knew which doors he meant. They were designed to pull across a portion of the room so as to make a separate dining place for a private party.

"I was there when it happened." His lower lip trembled, and his look of fear grew more intense. "I heard him scream."

"But you didn't see it happen, did you?" She offered him another of Polly's good oatmeal cookies, but he never noticed, so she set the plate down again. His eyes were set, as if looking at something far away.

It wasn't that she believed Anthony incapable of doing something so terrible. For Aaron's sake, and for Amanda's, she would like to think he would stop short of murder.

"I think Father killed Martin. I think he wants to kill me."

She leaned over and hugged him tight. "Never, Aaron. He wouldn't do that. He's your father."

"But he doesn't like me. He never liked me, and I don't think he liked my mother, either." His eyes were filled with apprehension. "Grandmother never liked her either. She never talked good about her. She always said, 'good riddance.' I think my father killed her, too."

"Now, Aaron . . ." she began, wanting to assure him that what he was saying was improbable.

Aaron took a long drink of his milk. "Martin didn't jump, Laine. Before he screamed I heard him holler, 'No, no'. Ask Emma. She saw Father."

"He was there," Emma admitted later when Elaine went to her room to question her.

"Did you talk to him?"

"Are you kidding? I didn't let him see me. He had just came up the stairs when I came back out of the dining area from checking out a table. I was glad I'd hid Aaron behind those doors, or who knows what might have happened?"

"Sills never tried to talk to you either?"

Emma shook her head. "I never even knew he was around until someone said his name after he was pronounced dead and they'd checked his billfold for identification."

Pauline fixed a light supper, clucking reprovingly about the events of the day.

Veronica, loathe it seemed to go to her apartment, told her husband, "Eat what Pauline's fixed. I guess we're family, too."

Irving never answered, but sat down at the table in the family dining room. Veronica hurried to an empty chair beside Mitchell. Irving glared at her and stabbed at his food with his fork.

Elaine took a seat between the children. She tried to speak of light subjects, but it was difficult not to think of the events of the day.

Why would Anthony shove Martin down over the railing? He depended on Martin. Martin was his 'yes man.' He did Anthony's bidding no matter what that included.

Mitchell carried on most of the table conversation, aiming his banter at Amanda who giggled at his nonsense. He ignored Veronica. That his lack of attention was deliberate was obvious even to her.

The children went to bed early. Amanda closed her eyes

and went to sleep almost at once, but Aaron had more dif-
ficulty in dropping off. Elaine left his light on and stayed
by his side until finally he slept.

Aaron's and Amanda's beds were empty when Elaine got
up the next morning. Until yesterday she had become unconcerned when the children left the house before she was
up and about. Today she felt uneasy. She told herself that
it was absurd to be this anxious, and that truth was borne
out the minute she entered the kitchen.

"Of course the kids are okay, Elaine," Pauline said in
her easy casual way. "But I understand your worrying,
that's for sure, what with that poor man dying right in front
of your eyes." She clucked sympathetically. "I'm glad I
didn't go. Russ wanted me to, but I told him to go on by
himself. I'd rather relax."

"I didn't see it happen," Elaine corrected.

"Oh. I guess it was the others . . ."

"Emma was close by. She was there right after it happened, I think. And Aaron, too. But I don't think anyone
actually saw him fall."

Pauline was carefully measuring flour into a large blue
bowl. "I hope it doesn't traumatize the boy. That could give
a grown person nightmares." She put the flour away and in
a detached, indifferent manner asked, "By the way, where
was Veronica while all of this was going on?" She mea-
sured sugar into a glass measuring cup.

"Veronica?" Elaine frowned. "I think she was waiting
for Irving somewhere."

"So she says." Pauline's lips became a thin line of disapproval as she busied herself with the electric beaters.
"Aaron, poor dear, thinks the man was pushed. I don't
know why he is so sure of that."

"Oh, I hoped I'd convinced him otherwise." Elaine was
so sure that what she said to Aaron had persuaded him he
must be mistaken.

"I'm just telling you what he said when he ate breakfast this morning. He said he'd heard the man scream."

Carefully, Elaine set her coffee cup down in the saucer. "I've heard that everyone screams when they fall. "Did Amanda hear what Aaron said?"

"My goodness, no. Aaron's got more sense than that. He waited until she'd gone outside with Emma."

"The police at Fulton Falls seemed to think it was suicide," she told Pauline.

"Easier for them that way." Pauline's opinion of the police was obvious. "You didn't have to give a statement?"

"No. I wasn't in the building at the time. Mandy and I had stopped to feed the ducks. But the others did, I guess . . . Mitchell and Laurie Lee, and Emma. Veronica, I suppose."

"Then Veronica was with the others?"

"She said she waited by the art gallery for Irving for awhile."

Pauline shook her head reproachfully. "She gives Irving a bad time. She threatens to find another man if he doesn't find a way to take her to Florida to live. Let her go, I say. And good riddance."

The telephone rang.

Pauline answered and said, "Just a moment." She held it out toward Elaine. "It's for you."

"For me?" Could Lyle be returning her call already? "Hello," she spoke into the mouthpiece wondering what he might have learned.

"Hello, my dear wife." Anthony's voice purred in her ear.

Chapter Thirteen

Elaine drew in a long and shaky breath.

"Hello, Anthony."

"How are my children?" His voice was dangerously pleasant.

"Is this a friendly call, Anthony?"

"My dear, what else?"

"You tell me."

"I would like to pick Aaron up sometime today."

"What makes you think he's with me?"

"Don't be childish. I've seen him. I've been told."

"Your messenger is dead."

"I know. Poor Martin." He was unemotional. "And while I'm there, I'll just pick up Amanda, too."

"You're not fit to be their father."

"And you are? A kidnapper?"

"A technical point."

"Yes, technical. The law rises and falls on technicalities."

Her hand tightened around the phone. She carried it with her out to the back patio. *Dare she tell him what Aaron claimed to have seen to get Anthony to back off? Or would that put Aaron in jeopardy? More than he was already in?* She needed time to think things through.

"A technical point can be murder," she suggested calmly.

"Martin?" His laugh was short and without mirth. "My dear, let me assure you that wasn't my doing."

"No, I mean what Aaron saw . . . what Sills did."

Again that soft mirthless laugh as he answered, "The imagination of children never ceases to amaze me. I can assure you that Roger is well, and having a wonderful time in Hawaii."

"I'm not sure I believe you . . . about Sills. You might have wanted him out of the way so he couldn't testify against you if I brought this case up in court. Leave us alone, Anthony, or I'll see to it that it does."

"Elaine, anytime you want to involve the law, go ahead. The law gives me no real problems. I can tell you who I think killed him. I heard him holler as I came up the stairs at the Circle Inn. I intended to grab Aaron, but there were so many people around I didn't get to. What does Aaron say happened?"

"He doesn't. He didn't see it either." She was trying to blend what he was telling her with what Aaron and Emma said, but her mind was in a muddle.

"Well, it wasn't me. I'll miss Martin. I depended on him, but he isn't the only one I depend on. I have other . . . friends." There was an underlying threat in his words.

"I have friends, too," she retorted, but her hand on the receiver was trembling.

"And I know most of them very well," he said softly. "Perhaps even better than you. I'll be seeing you soon, or at least . . . the children. Soon." The telephone clicked in her ear. The line hummed.

She cut the connection and sank, quaking, into a chair on the patio. Anthony's words both puzzled and terrified her. His quiet voice was no true indication of his emotion or his intent. During the last few years she'd learned that the quieter he spoke, the greater his anger. When he said he knew her friends well, she felt certain that he was speaking the truth. Anthony never felt the necessity to lie.

He seemed to be strangely unruffled by the death of Sills.

A half hour later Emma and Laurie Lee returned from their morning walk and found her still sitting there. They both settled down in padded lounging chairs, looking much better than on the evening before.

After a few moments Elaine broached the subject that was uppermost on her mind, one that now, after talking to Anthony, gave her cause for even greater urgency to be gone.

"I'm supposed to be leaving tomorrow, Laurie Lee. Have you made any definite arrangements yet?"

"Emma tells me you fear that your husband will try to take the children from you. If so, don't you think you'd be better off right here among your friends?"

Was that all Emma said? Had she mentioned to Laurie Lee that she had no right at all to take Aaron?

"What have you been saying, Emma?" Elaine bristled.

"Just that you're afraid Anthony will snatch the children. Don't be upset, Elaine. I agree with you, the quicker you get gone to Los Angeles, the better."

Laurie Lee placed a reassuring hand on her arm.

"I called Los Angeles and told Marge Snow, she's the office manager out there, to find a decent place for you. I didn't tell her to hurry, but I can if you wish, Elaine."

"I wish, and thank you, Laurie Lee. I really appreciate it." Elaine managed to smile as she got up out of her chair. "I think I'd best check on those kids again."

She found them with Mitchell, deeply enthralled by newly hatched chicks.

"Are they getting in your hair?" she wondered.

He grinned. "Not at all. They're getting to be quite the poultry experts."

*   *   *

Tuesday came and went. This was the day she had hoped that she and the children would be heading west, but she knew that most people didn't do business over the weekend. She just needed patience. Still, when one was worried about the well being of one's children, patience was a virtue not necessarily cultivated.

She'd heard no more from Anthony. She knew better than to believe he'd given up. Now she didn't know who his underlings might be, who she should watch for, what they looked like.

On Wednesday she happened to be in the kitchen when the telephone rang. Pauline, elbow deep in bread dough, nodded to her to get it. Veronica, sullen as usual, was preparing pans for baking.

She answered, her heart fluttering in her throat for fear Anthony might be calling her again.

"Laurie Lee's residence," she said.

"May I speak to Laurie Lee, please? Tell her it's Marge Snow."

"She's outside just now. She and Emma are taking a walk. May I take a message, or have her call you?"

She waited anxiously, hoping the call concerned when she could start working out there. Again she carried the phone out to the patio.

"Yes. Just tell her that I have the results of the sales meeting last night. When I talked to her yesterday she wanted to know the outcome."

"I'll tell her."

"To whom am I talking?" The voice was curious, but friendly.

"Elaine Webster. I'm the house guest here that you're finding a job for."

"Job? What job?"

"The one Laurie Lee called about. For me."

"Must have been one of the other girls. I don't really

handle the employment end. Anyway, ask Laurie Lee to give me a ring at her earliest convenience."

Elaine hung up as the connection was broken, but she didn't move away. She stared down at the phone and wondered if she was imagining things.

Hadn't Laurie Lee said she talked to Marge Snow? Elaine was positive that was the woman's name. Otherwise, Elaine thought, how would she even know that name?

She reentered the house, deep in troubled thoughts, and met Veronica coming out with a spray bottle of window cleaner in one hand and a roll of paper towels in the other.

Veronica eyed her morosely. "I thought you were supposed to be gone to California by now?"

"I did intend to," Elaine said, clipping off her words brusquely. Why did Veronica bring out the worst in her? She knew that Veronica rated very low in Pauline's eyes. In fact she said all Veronica really wanted was someone with money . . . someone who could take her to Florida to live.

She was always eyeing Mitchell but he never seemed to seek her company, at least not when anyone was around. And the more she knew Russ the more she was certain he wasn't interested in her either. He and Polly seemed to genuinely respect each other.

Noticing what Veronica carried she said, "Have the children been marking up the windows with fingerprints again?"

"Do you doubt it? When are you leaving?"

Elaine resented her belligerent attitude. She didn't have to answer her. Although Veronica was a relative of Laurie Lee's by marriage to her cousin, did that give her the right to be rude? She didn't think it was necessary to give her an answer, and didn't.

"I'm sorry about the windows, Veronica," was all she said. "I'll tell the children to be more careful."

"Well, there's enough to do getting ready for the Pow-Wow without doing the work a second time."

"You're absolutely right," Elaine agreed. "I'll tell them."

As Veronica went out she heard Irving come up to her on the other side of the door.

"What have you been doing?"

"Washing windows."

"Not earlier you weren't. I was looking all over for you. If I thought you were messing around . . ."

"What would you do, Mr. Big?"

Elaine, aware suddenly that she was eavesdropping, went back into the kitchen.

"At it again, are they?" Pauline shook her head in disapproval.

"Irving seems to have a jealous streak."

Pauline nodded. "With good reason. That Veronica leads him on a merry chase. She's a sly one, that's for sure." She set a huge stainless steel bowl of apples down in the sink. "If I was Irving, I'd shake her off like dust on my feet. She's always wantin' more than she has. Thinks Laurie Lee owes them, thinks she should set them up independently somewhere just because they're cousins. Doesn't see why she has to 'slave' here." Polly's voice took on a whining tone, mimicking Veronica. "I think Irving was even jealous of my old man at one time." She laughed heartily. "Can you picture that? Veronica and Russ?"

"Russ is a good-looking man, Polly."

Pauline chuckled. "I'll tell him that. He'll get a kick out of that."

"Have you got something I can do, Polly? I'm bored stiff with sitting around."

"Bored, are you? Well, I don't know. I don't reckon you want to peel apples? I'm making lots of apple bread and tarts."

For over an hour Elaine stood at the sink and peeled

apples while Pauline sliced or chopped them in her preparation of making the sweet bread and tarts.

"Enough," Polly said finally. "I'll freeze these and have
that much done for the Pow-Wow. We'll have these for a
brunch the first day. Try one."

Elaine did, and groaned appreciatively. "I don't know
how you get everything done, Polly."

"Well, it does take a lot of work and, of course, careful
planning. We always hire a couple of extra girls to help
while the Pow-Wow is going on.

"What else can I do?" Elaine looked expectantly around
the kitchen.

"Haven't you done enough? Well, you can carry that
trash can out to Veronica. She was supposed to come right
back in and do that an hour ago. Tell her to get back in
here."

"She might take offense if I say that."

Pauline grinned. "Tell her, 'Polly said so.' "

Elaine carried the trash out toward the back where Veronica was standing near the gate, intent in a discussion
with Mitchell. Veronica had wrapped her hands around the
gate post, her slim body swaying from side to side, her full
skirt swishing around bare legs, and smiling coquettishly
up into Mitchell's face.

Elaine banged the can down, jiggling some papers out
onto the grass as the can toppled, threatening to tip over.
She grabbed for it, righted it and stooped to pick up whatever spilled out. The return address on an envelope caught
her attention.

The address belonged to the newspaper where she had
written for information last week. The little window on the
envelope through which the addressee's name and location
was supposed to show revealed that the envelope was
empty. *Who could have opened her mail and destroyed the
contents without telling her?*

Chapter Fourteen

Elaine examined the contents of the trash. The can always stood in a corner near the back entry. Anyone could have tossed it in there. There was no sign of a letter.

She kept watching for Emma and Laurie Lee to return from their walk. They came in, carrying flowers from the garden.

"Marge Snow called. She wants you to call her," Elaine said, watching Laurie Lee for some change of expression. There was none.

"Thank you." Laurie Lee concentrated on arranging the flowers in a round white ceramic container.

"She said she didn't know anything about finding me a job."

Laurie Lee's eyes flashed. Her smile faded.

"She probably forgot. Perhaps I didn't stress the hurry." She smiled artlessly and turned to insert another flower in just the right spot. "I really want you to stay for the Pow-Wow. I've been telling the children all about the music and dancing. I think Aaron especially might get a kick out of watching. I'll definitely get everything taken care of after this is all over. Am I forgiven?"

What could Elaine say. There was nothing underhanded,

really, in what Laurie Lee did or didn't do. Everyone had been exceptionally busy with the upcoming event.

"I just think it would be good for you to be here, sort of a crasher course in our product." Laurie Lee held up the finished bouquet to admire.

By Saturday everything had been spruced up for the Pow-Wow. The pheasant pens were neat and tidy, the yard had been close-clipped, and water sparkled in the blue pool behind the house. All was ready.

With the incident of Marge Snow in her mind, Elaine had forgotten to mention to Laurie Lee or to Emma about the letter from the newspaper. She caught up with Emma just as her friend was going into her room to get ready to receive guests.

"I've been expecting a letter from Chicago." Elaine got right to the point. "Have you seen it?"

Emma pulled open her closet door. "Haven't seen it. You might check with Polly."

"I found the envelope in the wastebasket yesterday. Someone had removed the letter and threw the envelope away."

"Why would anyone do that? Here, what do you think? This dress, or this one?" She held up two for Elaine's approval. "I never can decide." The letter was dismissed as unimportant.

"I wrote to the newspaper where that picture was published. Remember? The one we were looking at in Laurie Lee's room that day?"

"Why would you write to them?" Emma kept the white summery frock in one hand and hung the navy blue back in the closet.

"I wanted information about the clipping. Who was in the photo, and why it was in the paper. You said you'd saved it, but if you did that, why was it Laurie Lee who hung onto it?"

"What are you trying to say, Elaine?"

"I'm saying the letter was meant for me. Why would anyone take my letter and not let me see it? It doesn't make sense."

"You're right." Emma smiled innocuously, and turned back to her closet, putting an end to the discussion.

Upon reaching the downstairs, Elaine was enticed to enter the kitchen. Tantalizing aromas drifted out into the hall. Curiosity took her to the extra refrigerators near the back door in the rear entry.

Nibblers awaited on the top shelves, trays of fresh fruit, preserved and sugared. There were relishes covered with clear plastic wrap, celery, green onions, pickles, and olives. Tiny spicy beets were in a dark green bowl and radish roses and carrot curls were in other bowls packed in ice and covered with more plastic wrap. Salads shimmered in colorful glory.

Pauline noticed Elaine admiring her work and beamed her pleasure. "There'll be hot food that we'll be making throughout the day," she said, her eyes on one of her helpers who was arranging finger food on a tray.

"Who will eat it all?"

"There'll be a crowd here early enough to get in on my cinnamon rolls and coffee," she replied confidently.

"So that's what smells so good. I'd better get to Los Angeles before I get fat."

"This Pow-Wow is for the distributors and their spouses who have reached a certain spot on the totem pole. Laurie Lee likes to reward them with this huge blowout."

Elaine went to find Aaron and Amanda. Aaron grumbled at having to clean up, but Amanda relished in wearing a new dress that Emma got for her for the occasion. She reminded them to be polite, to stay clean, and for Aaron to keep an eye on his little sister.

Cars were rolling down the lane by nine just as Polly predicted. Big cars, little cars, vans, pickup trucks, bugs and limos. They filled the open space beyond the fenced yard and the pheasant pens.

Elaine's astonishment grew. She hadn't dreamed so many people would respond to Laurie Lee's invitations.

"You were right, Polly," Elaine told her.

"They aren't coming just to hear the speakers," Polly said, smiling. "They look forward to this day."

"Elaine." A cheerful voice called when she left the kitchen. She turned to see Lyle Shubin in a navy blazer, gray slacks, and a sport shirt open at the neck. He gathered her hands in his own, and bending forward, kissed her on the cheek.

"Lyle," she responded enthusiastically, surprising even herself at how glad she was to see him. "I never even thought about you being here."

"I'm a distributor now, and half way up on the totem pole. You're looking great."

"You, too."

"Admit it," he chided. "You've all but forgotten me."

"Never. Didn't I call you a few days ago?"

A shadow crossed his face. "Sure," he said, still holding her hands. "You remember me when you want something."

"I am sorry. I know I promised to keep in touch, and I did think of you."

"What did you think?" He moved closer until their shoulders were touching. "Good thoughts or bad? Come on, now, confess."

"Lyle, you fool. Can't you be serious?"

He sobered. "Sure I can. I'd like to be serious with you. Just let me know when."

She pulled away, laughing lightly. "Well, right now, let's do some serious eating. You'll never believe all the good things the cook has been making."

At her suggestion they carried rolls and coffee out to the back patio. She was anxious to learn what he found out concerning Roger Reams, but she didn't want to appear as if that was her only reason for showing interest in him. Part of the seats and benches, and the chairs under bright umbrellas were already filling. Even the pool held early swimmers, splashing and calling out to one another.

A long-legged blonde was sunning herself near the diving board. She rolled over lazily and looked up at Lyle from under long, thick eyelashes.

"Why, hel-lo, Lyle," she said, stretching out to her best angle.

"Hello, Felicia."

"When you get done stuffing yourself, come sit by me and I'll put some sunscreen on you." She raised a hand and flipped long golden hair over her suntanned shoulders.

"Later, Felicia. Don't burn that gorgeous skin, now."

She pouted as he walked on with Elaine.

"Let's go over there," Lyle suggested, nodding his head toward a table that had been positioned off by itself.

Finally, after discussing how successful Lyle had been in the business, and her intention of going on to Los Angeles, she let herself ask the question that had been burning uppermost in her mind.

"What did you find out about Roger Reams?"

Again a shadow crossed his face. He lowered his voice. "I almost got my neck in a noose. After I made inquiries, the law made inquiries of me. I had to come up with a good reason why I wanted to know."

"Why? What happened to him?"

"I told you that day you asked that he was a known hoodlum. Or was . . . as the case may be." He looked at her carefully. "The man is dead of causes unknown. The police found him in the river, his feet wearing a new style of shoes, cement shoes."

She could only stare at him.

"After I made inquiries, the police had my telephone tapped. I spent hours at the police station answering questions."

"But you had no reason to want him dead."

"Seems they had no one better to question. They let me go. Said they had no eyewitnesses, and couldn't hold me with the little they had to go on."

"Eyewitnesses?" *Wasn't Aaron an eye witness?*

"Eyewitnesses."

She started to respond, then stopped. She must never say a word, nor trust anyone, not even Lyle. Aaron had evidently been right, and she needed to keep that information from becoming common knowledge.

Was that the real reason Anthony wanted to get Aaron back in his keeping? Anthony wouldn't harm his own son . . . not physically. *She was sure of that, wasn't she?* He probably wanted him where no one would have access to him—at least until he had him convinced that he never saw what he had seen.

She continued to talk nonsense with Lyle, but her mind was elsewhere.

Even if Anthony merely wanted Aaron back to keep him quiet, what kind of life would that be for the boy? When she tried to downplay in her own mind the extent Anthony might go in keeping the law out of his life, she found that she was uncertain of just what he would do. She was reminded of Martin Sills. *Had his death been a retaliation of something gone wrong? Was Anthony solely responsible, or had an unknown hit man taken care of Sills?*

"It's been so good to talk to you, Lyle, but I really must go see about the children."

"Children? I thought you only had a little girl?"

He was smiling at her strangely, or was she beginning to distrust everyone?

"Well . . ."

He laughed. "Don't look so stunned. Tales get around. I heard via the grapevine that you made off with Anthony's kid, too."

"Oh, Lyle, please don't tell anyone. Aaron is such a sweet little boy and he's actually afraid of his father."

"I don't wonder. I'm afraid of Anthony, myself."

She certainly wasn't going to mention that Aaron had seen Sills kill Roger Reams.

"Where is Aaron?"

"Oh, around." She was deliberately vague.

"Watch him," Lyle said lightly, but looking serious. "Remember what happened to Martin Sills."

"You heard? But of course you would."

"There was a very small item on the back page of the daily paper. But I hear a lot of talk. The paper said the police are investigating, which means, they'll look into it for a few days, and if nothing shows up, they'll figure one less hoodlum."

Elaine got up. "I must go. Go to the pool and find yourself a blonde."

She berated herself as she walked away. She should have cut all ties with anyone connected to Chicago. She vowed that once she got to Los Angeles she would leave and give no one her address. She'd go to another city. *But with no money at her disposal how was she going to make it on her own without the help that Laurie Lee offered?*

Her stomach fluttered with emptiness. She had never felt so alone. Managing by herself in a strange place didn't sound like fun, but if that meant safety for Aaron and Amanda, she could do it. She could and would do a lot just to keep them out of harm.

As she passed through the kitchen, Pauline, her face flushed from the heat, looked up and smiled.

"Everything okay?" she asked Elaine.

"As far as I know. The rolls were simply delicious. I'm looking for the children."

"I haven't seen them. Have you seen Veronica?"

"Not since early this morning."

Polly scowled. "If you do see her, tell her to get herself in here. She knows she's supposed to be helping me."

"I will if I see her. I'm going to see if the kids might be out by the pheasant pens. They like to watch the men at work."

Pauline mixed something in a bowl, beating almost viciously with a large spoon.

"So does Veronica," she muttered.

Chapter Fifteen

Aaron and Amanda were exactly where Elaine guessed they would be, out by the pheasant pens. They were standing well back from the fence so as not to get dirty from the dusty wire. Veronica was there, too, lounging against a gate, dressed in a white blouse and a full skirt of emerald green. Her eyes were turned to watch the men at work, even though they didn't appear to be paying all that much attention to her.

"We're keepin' clean, Laine," Aaron reassured her when she approached. He ran up to her so she could see for herself.

"They're pretty good kids," Veronica drawled, "as long as they stay away from my windows." She sounded almost cheerful.

Elaine looked directly at Veronica. "Polly asked me to tell you that she needs your help in the kitchen."

"Wow." Sarcasm filled Veronica's voice. Her eyes widened with exaggerated alarm. "I guess I'd better run right in and help ol' Polly." She made no move to go.

Elaine shrugged and turned away. "None of my business."

"Right. And none of my business that Aaron doesn't call

you 'mother.' " Veronica grinned wickedly and swirled her skirt while watching the men to see if they were watching her.

Irving limped over to the gate where she was standing. "Veronica, go back to the house where you belong."

"I belong where I choose to belong," she told him distinctly, not bothering to lower her voice.

Russ and Mitchell both glanced in her direction.

"I'm getting a little tired of this," Irving said.

"Then why not make arrangements for us to get out of here . . . go to Florida like you've been promising and promising?"

Elaine took the children by the hand and headed back toward the house, disturbed to hear that even Veronica had picked up on the fact that Aaron called her by name. God help her if Veronica learned under what circumstances he was brought to Iowa. She might be wondering about him, but there was no way she could know that Elaine brought him without permission. Unless someone told her. *But who would do that? Emma? Not likely. Emma didn't trust Veronica, and would never confide in her.*

Veronica didn't seem worried about Pauline needing help. When Elaine glanced back over her shoulder she saw that she was following her husband into the pens, and evidently had no intention of helping Polly.

"Wait up," Elaine heard a familiar voice call. She waited. "Where are you going?" Mitchell caught up with her.

"Back inside. I just came out to get the children." They fell in step. "Polly's fit to be tied. Veronica's supposed to be helping."

"Can't say that I blame Polly." Mitchell held the back door open for her. Just inside the entry he placed a hand on one arm and drew her to a halt. "Mother keeps telling me you're going to be leaving, but this morning she said she wasn't so sure. What's going on?"

"I wish I knew. I should have been on my way, but

Laurie Lee wanted me to wait until after the Pow-Wow. When she's good enough to make all the arrangements it's hard for me to insist that I leave immediately."

"Why are you going?" His voice was low. There was concern in his eyes. "And why the hurry?"

"I've never intended to stay here. This isn't my home. I'm just a guest."

"There's something more. I've got eyes. And ears. And remember, I've done the arithmetic. Veronica asked you, and now I am. Why doesn't Aaron call you 'mother?' "

"Lots of children call their parents by their names. It's none of Veronica's business."

"Nor mine?" He still held her arm.

She never answered, but made a move to pull away.

"Nor mine," he conceded, and dropped his hand to his side.

No sooner had she got the children settled at a table in the kitchen for lunch when Lyle came looking for her.

"Will you sit with me to eat, Elaine?" His brown eyes lit up when she accepted.

They filled their plates from the buffet and found a place at one of the small tables on the patio. A gentle breeze fluttered the bright tablecloths and rippled the umbrellas that were scattered across the yard to keep the hot sun off everyone.

Laurie Lee was everywhere, greeting newcomers, and stopping at various tables to chat with those who had arrived earlier. She made a beautiful picture in her bright blouse accented with Indian beads and her tan skirt with a fringe at the hem line. The Indian adornments looked simple yet sophisticated. Her dark hair combed into a braid was wound around her head. Even though the color was a perfect match, Elaine was sure the braid was a fake. Laurie Lee's hair was too short to make a braid.

Her face was glowing. She was enjoying this night where she reigned supreme.

Laurie Lee had specifically asked Elaine to attend the meeting in the basement over which she was presiding that afternoon. "You need to absorb all the information you can, if you're going to start working for me again."

Afterward, Elaine congratulated her on the presentation.

"Where's Aaron and Amanda?" Laurie Lee accepted the compliment as her just due.

"In the kitchen. Polly's keeping an eye on them."

Elaine felt guilty about leaving them with the work-harried Polly, but Polly had insisted, "Laurie Lee wants you to go to that meeting, Elaine. Besides, it will give me an excuse to sit down for a bit and still be able to keep my eye on what the girls are doing."

"With Polly?" Laurie Lee looked relieved. "That's all right then. Just be careful. There's such a crowd here. This shindig grows bigger every year." She smiled. "You're not worried about your ex with all this going on, are you?"

"Somewhat, but I try to keep an eye on them."

"Of course you do." Laurie Lee nodded her head.

"Is something bothering you, Laurie Lee?"

Laurie Lee gave a little laugh. "I'm a worry wart. Have you seen Emma?"

"Earlier. She was talking to Lyle Shubin."

On her way to the kitchen Elaine had noticed Emma standing in a flower-filled alcove in the front hall, absorbed in a conversation with Veronica and Irving. Veronica, looking gloomy and out of sorts, was listening intently to a conversation between her husband and Emma.

Elaine waited, not wanting to interrupt them. Veronica waved her hands in a gesture that seemed to protest something that Emma said. Glancing up they saw her standing by the door watching them, and quit talking. Irving and Veronica hurried off to the back of the house.

"That Veronica," Emma said, coming up to Elaine. "She thinks she shouldn't have to help. I told her all of my regulars here on the farm are working. That the party is for Laurie Lee's distributors."

"Laurie Lee seems nervous. You didn't tell her the truth about how I brought Aaron here, did you?"

Emma looked surprised. "Of course not."

"Well, she seems unusually concerned about the children. In fact, she was cautioning me to keep an eye on them."

"I imagine it was that deal with Martin Sills. That made everybody jumpy."

"Another thing, Mitchell told me that you weren't so sure about my going to Los Angeles. I've got to go somewhere, Emma. You know that. Someplace where no one knows me."

"I did tell Mitchell that. Laurie Lee told me she wished you'd just stay on here and help me with office details. She's taken to the children, you know. I think she feels that your staying here might be the answer to all of your problems. With us around you needn't worry so much."

Elaine sighed. "But she doesn't know he isn't my son. If it became public knowledge how I brought him, Laurie Lee would regret helping me. She would hate all the hoopla if it got out. If she knew she wouldn't want me to stay."

"Laurie Lee expects a lot," said a mocking voice behind them, and Elaine turned quickly to see Mitchell.

"Now, Mitch," Emma said. "Don't start knocking Laurie Lee. I won't allow it."

"You never would, Mother." He flashed her a winsome smile. "You never would."

Emma threw Elaine a smile back over her shoulder as she wound her arm through her son's, and walked away.

Polly was working again when Elaine reached the kitchen. The children were sitting quietly helping one of the girls fill glass relish trays. There was no sign of Veronica. So much for the talk Emma had with her.

"Do these people eat and drink all the time, Polly?"

"There'll be dancing later tonight," Pauline told her. "By then most of our duties will be done."

And dancing there was. No sooner had the evening buffet been cleared away when the band arrived and started setting up in the walk-in basement. Chairs from the afternoon meeting were now placed along the wall all around the room, and were rapidly being filled by people entering through the patio doors that opened onto the pool side, or by the inside stairs from the first floor above.

From the moment the music started Laurie Lee was whirled from one partner to another. The band played a mixture of ballroom dance music. The floor was never empty.

Elaine danced with Lyle several times and with Mitchell once. She had allowed Aaron and Amanda to come down and watch as long as they stayed in a certain area of the dimly lit room. She cautioned them again to not even go to the bathroom without coming to get her.

Each time she glanced in their direction they were sitting side by side, Aaron interested in what was going on, Amanda drooping a little.

"This Lyle fellow," Mitchell said, as they danced across the floor, "close friend of yours?"

"An old friend." She pondered her answer. *How close was close? Someone you could depend on? Someone who was there for you in times of trouble?* "Other than your mother, I have no close friends."

He laughed, and pressed his hand against the middle of her back, drawing her nearer. "Then let's get closer," he said.

She laughed and pulled back ever so slightly.

"Not that kind of close."

He danced with her out through the patio doors, leading her to a secluded spot behind a bush where the moon cast a shadow. He pulled her toward him and when she didn't pull away, he tipped up her chin.

Her lips waited for his kiss, her arms going up around his shoulders. The moment started out casual and seemed so natural, but she was shaken far more than she expected. She hadn't realized until then that she had hidden this desire to be held, to be kissed.

She accused herself of behaving like a flighty teenage girl. His embrace ended only because she moved back, dropping her arms at her sides.

"Was that too close?" He seemed reluctant to let her go.

Dare she trust even him? How well did she know him? How well did he know Anthony? Mitchell had worked in Chicago, too, the same time that his mother did. And Emma knew Anthony somehow. Mutual acquaintances, she'd confided.

"Thank you for the dance." Elaine backed primly away.

"Thank you for the kiss." His response was solemn, but in the near darkness she saw his suppressed smile.

"Don't mention it." She made an effort to sound light-hearted and carefree, but her heart pounded.

"A gentleman never does," he retorted.

They reentered the room together. He stopped her just outside the door to look directly into her face.

"Is my lipstick straight?" he asked.

She stifled a giggle. Before she could answer, Lyle came up, took her by the hand, and said, "This one is mine."

Lyle was an expert dancer. As he whirled her around the room in a lively waltz she noticed Emma and Laurie Lee start up the stairs together.

"That was exhilarating," she told Lyle as the dance ended.

"We'll have another go at it later," he promised.

Elaine looked over to the spot where the children had sat all evening. Amanda's head was drooping as she sat asleep, but the chair that Aaron occupied was empty.

She looked around, but he was nowhere in sight. He might have gone to the bathroom by himself in spite of her orders. She checked those downstairs. He wasn't there.

Elaine went over to Amanda and gave her a little shake. "Where's Aaron?"

"I don't know." Amanda sounded cross. Her body sagged down in the seat, her eyelids were heavy.

Elaine picked her up, carrying her up the stairs to the kitchen. Polly was still bumbling about. "Have you seen Aaron?"

"Not since you took him earlier."

"Maybe he's with Mitchell." Elaine stood Amanda down on her feet. "Come on, honey, let's go find your brother."

Amanda woke up when the cool night air hit her face, and walked willingly along, her hand clutched in Elaine's.

They circled the yard and pool, and came back to the front of the house. Laurie Lee brushed past her, seeming in a hurry. Elaine stopped her with a touch to her arm.

"Have you seen Aaron anywhere?"

"Aaron? He's been sitting beside Amanda all evening." She started to walk on.

"Maybe he's with Mitchell," Elaine surmised. How often since they came here had that been the case? *Of course*, she comforted herself. *That was it. He was with Mitchell.*

Elaine returned to the basement dance floor. The band was just returning from a break. Laurie Lee was speaking to the band leader as he got ready to take his place again. Someone else moved in to capture Laurie Lee's attention. Fewer dancers seemed to be participating. Mitchell was leading a young woman out onto the floor. Lyle was at the bar talking animatedly with a man Laurie Lee had hired to tend bar for the night.

But there was no sign of Aaron.

With Amanda in hand, Elaine headed for the kitchen. Pauline sat alone at the kitchen table, her chin in her hand, her elbow on the table. Her eyes were red. Obviously she had been weeping.

"Polly, what's wrong?"

"Veronica," said Polly darkly.

"What's she done now?"

"She told me that she and Russ had been together. You know."

"Oh, Polly, she didn't."

"I just can't believe it, Elaine. We've been married twenty-five years." Pauline sniffed. "She thinks we've got money put away."

"You can't believe a word she's saying, Polly. You know how she is. I hate to leave you like this but I've just got to find Aaron."

"You go along. Don't pay me no mind."

"Have you seen Emma?"

"Not for awhile."

Elaine took Amanda back down to the basement. She kept telling herself that Aaron was with Emma somewhere. She saw that Laurie Lee was dancing with Lyle.

As soon as the music stopped Laurie Lee came toward her. "Have you found Aaron?"

"No. And I don't know where Emma is. Surely he must be with her."

Laurie Lee closed her eyes. When she opened them Elaine saw in them the dread and fear that surely reflected her own. Laurie Lee's next words did nothing to banish that fear.

"Oh, Elaine, Lyle just told me that Anthony is here . . . here at the Pow-Wow. He saw him standing out by the pheasant pens."

"Anthony?" Elaine was shaken. *How could Laurie Lee know him well enough to speak his name so casually? He'd been a stockholder, true. But that had been years ago.*

Coldness touched the back of her neck, and tingled down

her spine. She turned to go up the stairs, dragging a protesting Amanda along. Her feet didn't want to carry her
fast enough. She wanted to run, but she resisted the impulse.

Anthony here? And Aaron nowhere in sight? Grabbing
Amanda up in her arms she rushed with her out into the
cool dark night.

Chapter Sixteen

"He's got to be with Emma," Elaine said, over and over again, trying to reassure herself as much as anyone. She looked everywhere around the yard and around the pool, and in the pool.

"Yes," Amanda said suddenly. "Aaron's with Emma. She came and got him."

Elaine stopped and looked down at her small daughter in wonder.

"What did you say?"

"Emma wanted to show him something." Amanda was breathless and becoming more crabby with each passing minute. She was tired of being jostled in her mother's arms, then, almost dragged all over the yard.

"Oh, Amanda, why didn't you say so when I first asked you?" Relief made her suddenly weak.

"I forgetted," Amanda said sorrowfully. "Emma wouldn't take me, 'cause I was too little." Her lower lip trembled with hurt feelings. She was tired of being too little.

"She didn't say what she wanted to show him?" Elaine was puzzled.

Amanda shook her head.

125

Mitchell caught up with them, his white shirt showing up gradually in the dark like a moonflower opening on the vine.

"Laurie Lee says you're worried about Aaron."

"I was. I am. Laurie Lee said Lyle Shubin told her that he'd seen Anthony out by the pheasant pens. But if Emma has Aaron with her, I'm sure he's okay."

"Where'd they go, Amanda?" Mitchell bent over the small girl.

"Emma had something to show him." She yawned.

"Probably Emma saw Anthony and wanted to hide Aaron." Elaine started on in the direction she'd been going.

Laurie Lee joined them. "What's wrong?"

Mitchell drew Elaine to a stop. "Quit playing games, Elaine. Most people aren't in such a tizzy as you seem to be half the time. What's wrong? Why would Mother hide Aaron?"

"I'm not playing games." Elaine tried to hide her irritation at his manner, his words. "I truly think that if Anthony has his way he will not only take Aaron away, but Amanda, too. I'd be lucky to ever see either of them again."

"Surely he wouldn't be that mean?"

"You don't know Anthony."

"Surely he has feelings. He's their father. He wouldn't do anything to hurt them."

"What do you know about what he would or wouldn't do? You can't even begin to know."

"Who would deprive a child from his mother?"

"Anthony would."

He must have seen something in her eyes or on her face that showed her pain, her fear, for he swung Amanda up in his arms and started out across the yard. "Let's find Aaron," he said.

Polly stood by the corner of the house. When she heard they were still looking for Aaron, she said, "Why not leave Amanda with me? The poor little thing is worn out."

"Keep her right with you, Pauline," Laurie Lee cautioned.

"Every minute," Polly promised.

"I'm coming along," Laurie Lee said. "I'm tired of dancing. Everytime I stop some fellow thinks it's his duty to dance with me. I'm worn out."

They all followed Mitchell toward the pheasant pens.

Before they reached them they heard a loud commotion and screeching like Elaine had never heard before. A dark clothed figure stumbled out of the pen, and rushed past them, moaning in pain and anger.

It was Anthony. He faced them, coming to an abrupt standstill.

"Little brat," he said, and pulled a white square from his pocket to wipe his face. Dark blotches stained the handkerchief, showing up even in the moonlight. He swore aloud and started to walk away.

"Wait." Mitchell sounded angry.

Anthony walked faster to where his car was parked in the shadows of the farmyard driveway.

"Anthony," Elaine hollered, too. But Anthony didn't stop. He yanked the door open, jumped in, and was gone, the motor roaring as he fishtailed out and down the lane.

"What was he doing in the pheasant pens?" Mitchell wondered.

Elaine glanced around uncertainly, unsure now that Aaron was safe somewhere with Emma.

"Aaron," she called.

From the pen came a hesitant answer, "Laine, is that you?"

"Oh, Aaron." Elaine looked about anxiously. "Where are you?"

"Is Father gone?"

"He's gone. Come on out."

From somewhere within the pen a small shadow separated from the dark background and moved toward them.

Mitchell opened the gate, and Aaron ran through and into Elaine's arms.

"I was so scared," he said. Elaine put her arms around him, feeling his shoulders quiver and shake.

"You're all right now, Aaron," she consoled, and vowed silently that he would never be taken from her to be raised by a father so feared.

"What happened?" she asked gently as they all gathered around him in the moonlight.

"Father wanted me to go with him. I told him I couldn't and he got mad. He tried to get me to go into the house and get Amanda, but I wouldn't." He hiccupped. His voice deepened as he mocked his father's voice. " 'Are you afraid of me, Boy?' When I said I was, he laughed at me. So I ran into the pen. I wasn't afraid of the pheasants."

"Where's Emma?" Elaine asked. "What were you two doing out here anyway?"

"Well, Amanda was going to sleep, and Emma said she wanted to show me something. She went over to the feed shed to get it, and left me by the gate to the pheasant pen. Right then, I saw Father sneaking up on me, so I opened the gate and ran in."

"Where's my mother now?" Mitchell wondered, and looked around.

"Maybe she saw Anthony and was trying to lure him away so he wouldn't see Aaron," Laurie Lee suggested. "Maybe she's gone back to the house looking for us, and we're out here looking for her."

"What's everyone doing out here?" A familiar voice came toward them out of the dark shadows.

"Veronica, what are you doing?" Laurie Lee demanded.

"Well, now, dear cousin," Veronica drawled. "I'm gettin' a bit of fresh air. Is that against the law?"

Laurie Lee's breath caught at Veronica's rudeness. "Have you seen Emma?"

"Last time I saw her was when I was dancing with Mitchell. Right, Mitch?" She stared at Mitchell coyly.

"We couldn't find Aaron, but he's okay. Now, we're wondering where Emma is," Elaine explained.

"You say she went to the feed shed, Aaron?" Mitchell asked the boy patiently, ignoring Veronica's direct question.

"That's where she said she had the surprise. She went to get it. Maybe she's having trouble getting it. Maybe it's something really big."

"I think I'll just run over there and have a look." Mitchell decided.

"I was in the pen, so I really couldn't see where she went. Every time Father tried to come in the pen I grabbed an ol' pheasant and threw it at him. Some of them ol' birds raked him good, Mitch. But I learned how to grab them."

Mitchell laughed, patted Aaron on the back, and said, "Attaboy." He strode away toward the shed. The others followed. He opened the door and reached for the light switch.

"Mother," he called. "Mother."

Elaine waited with the others just outside the door.

"I'll bet she's gone to the house," Veronica drawled.

Elaine doubted that. *Emma wouldn't return to the house without taking Aaron with her, would she?*

Before she could voice her opinion, Mitchell came back to the door, one hand groping the side of the door jamb. He was swaying drunkenly from side to side.

They rushed toward him, but he blocked the way.

"Mitch. What is it?" Elaine cried.

He leaned against the partition as if he couldn't stand without support. "Oh, God. I can't believe it." His voice was cracked with emotion, and he seemed about to collapse. "She's . . . she's dead. My . . . my mother's dead."

Elaine and Laurie Lee both pressed forward, and would have gone inside, but he wouldn't let them get past.

"No, no." He shook his head from side to side as if trying to shake off some horror he'd just seen. "She's dead, I tell you. Get Russ. Get Irving, but don't go in."

"I'll go." Veronica took off running toward the house.

"She can't be dead, Mitchell." Elaine felt as though she were in a long tunnel. There was a roaring in her ears that told her this was not real, that she hadn't heard what she thought she'd heard.

"Maybe we can help." Laurie Lee touched his arm gently.

He shook her off. "She's dead, I tell you. Her head . . ." He choked, unable to go on.

Russ and Irving came rushing out immediately. With their help, Laurie Lee and Elaine guided Mitchell out of the doorway, and over to the wooden gate that led into the pheasant pen.

Aaron was clinging to Elaine, and she turned her attention to him, leaving Laurie Lee to cope with Mitchell who was sagging against the gate.

Pauline came out carrying Amanda and suggested she take Aaron back to the house. "The doctor is on his way," she announced. "Why don't all of you come on in the house?"

"Go on, Mitch," Russ said kindly. "I'll stay with her."

They made their way in to the family living room, collapsing into chairs to wait for the doctor's report.

"I can't believe it." Elaine was on the edge of hysteria.

The doctor's voice was filled with regret when he came in. "I'm sorry," he began. "There was nothing I could do."

Mitchell, white and sick, sat at the table, looking down at his trembling hands as though they didn't belong to him. Laurie Lee went with the doctor to contend with the guests.

"No one must leave until the sheriff gets here," he was telling Laurie Lee as they left the room.

The sheriff faced them all gravely when he came in after his initial investigation. The guests had all been herded down into the basement to gather in clusters. They commented on what had occurred, drank more coffee than they wanted to, and ate the snacks that Polly put out for them.

"Accidental, I'm sure," the sheriff told the family still gathered in the family dining room. "The tool rack is next to a partition, and as she fumbled around in the dark . . . you did say that you put the light on, didn't you?" The question was directed at Mitchell. At his nod, the sheriff continued, "I think the crowbar fell down and hit her on the back of the head."

"I don't believe that for one minute." Elaine was vehement with outrage that Emma's death should be passed off as accidental. "My husband was here. Check him out before you dismiss this so easily."

The sheriff regarded her wearily as if she was merely caught up in the emotion of the event and should be handled delicately.

"I want to talk to the guests. Come along, Brian." He left the room with his deputy, saying, "I want all of their home addresses and telephone numbers and where they work. Don't leave anyone out."

"What did she go to the shed for?" Elaine wondered.

"I didn't even look." Mitchell passed a hand over his eyes. "And now probably everything is all stirred up by the officers and we'll never know."

"Mitchell, I'm sorry." Veronica's voice was a little too sad, too pitying. She placed one hand on his arm.

He winced and said, "Thank you."

Even though Elaine was sick at heart at Emma's death she couldn't help but feel a pang of gratefulness that at least Aaron had been kept safe.

Laurie Lee had gone up to her room, helped by Pauline. Elaine lay awake a long time, acutely aware of the empty room across the hall, of the emptiness in all of their lives.

Aaron cried out once in his sleep, and she sat beside him, his hand in hers, until he fell asleep again.

The next morning he awoke early and came over to her bed. "Do you think Father killed Emma, Laine? Just like he killed my mother and Martin?"

"The sheriff thinks it was an accident, Aaron. We'll just have to wait for them to complete the investigation."

He crawled under the covers beside her, and fell back to sleep even before she did.

Someone was gone from her life that had been there for years. Someone who had always seemed concerned for her well being. One thought plagued her: Would this have happened had she not come here seeking refuge?

She slept, finally. The sun was slanting in through her windows when she awakened. Dressed, and dreading the day ahead, she hurried down the back stairs.

"There's coffee ready, Elaine." Pauline was at her side with a cup and saucer.

"Thanks, Polly." She carried it to the table in the family dining room.

"Can I fix you . . ."

"No, nothing." She shuddered.

"Why not try a little fruit? It's iced and good for that queasy feeling." She placed a goblet of cubed cantaloupe and sliced red plums in front of her.

"Are you sure?" Elaine looked up at her and smiled.

"Tried it myself," Polly said.

It was then that Elaine noticed the eyes that were too bright, the mouth tremulous. She'd been feeling so sorry for herself that she hadn't really stopped to think how deeply Polly might be affected by Emma's death. *Or was Polly's sad countenance due, at least in part, to Veronica's words the night before? Had that just been last night? How far away and long ago that seemed.*

She patted Pauline's hand. "We're all going to miss Emma," she said. If Pauline wished to claim any other reason for her sadness that was up to her.

Pauline sniffed. "I feel so sorry for Laurie Lee, poor

dear. She and Emma have been exceptionally close over the years. She relied on Emma even more than she realized, I think. There's nothing they wouldn't do for one another."

"How is she doing?"

"I sat with her for most of the night. She seemed almost afraid to close her eyes."

"You should have called me."

"I asked her if I should, and she said you had your hands full enough with the children."

"Yes. Aaron was restless, too."

"Bless his heart. I felt sure he would be. He and Emma had become quite close."

Elaine knew that to be true. When they first came here, Emma had been less than enthusiastic about Aaron's presence, but she'd put that aside and made him welcome.

"Where is Laurie Lee now?"

"Out on the patio with Mitchell." Polly, shaking her head sympathetically, went back into the kitchen.

Elaine dreaded what she needed to do next . . . see Laurie Lee and Mitchell. Mitchell's face bore the strain of last night's tragedy, but he was calm and in control. Laurie Lee, on the other hand, seemed on the verge of hysteria. She was pale, and although she tried to control her tears, she sobbed as she talked.

Elaine found herself in the position of being a consoler. She said a lot of words—on disconnected issues—being brisk one minute and ready to break down the next.

When she got up to leave to get the children out of bed, Mitchell got up, too.

"You've comforted us, Elaine. Who's shoulder are you crying on?" She shook her head, indicating there had been none available. He took a step toward her, and with Laurie Lee looking on, he folded her in his arms.

"Go ahead and cry," he soothed, and her tears flowed in spite of herself.

* * *

Emma was buried in a plot in a cemetery near Fulton Falls. Until Elaine heard others discuss her life, she hadn't realized that not only had Emma graduated from high school at Fulton Falls, but that Laurie Lee had, too.

"That's where they got acquainted . . . in school," Mitchell told her.

Elaine sat with him and Laurie Lee on the patio the day after Emma's funeral.

"She was always such a go-getter, and I the shy one," Laurie Lee reminisced. "I could always count on Emma to help me over the rough spots."

"Then you surely find solace in knowing she felt the same way about you," Elaine said.

"I might have made her life a little more secure, but she gave of herself . . ." Her voice broke off. After a moment she got herself under control again. She smiled at Elaine. "You're very much like her in some ways, you know. I appreciate so much your being here just now." She squeezed one of Elaine's hands.

During the following week Elaine was called on to do more and more in helping Laurie Lee with small matters, in making minor decisions.

When Elaine mentioned she had to leave soon, Laurie Lee looked at her helplessly.

"Oh, no. You can't go. I'd miss the children so much. Mitchell has agreed to stay on for awhile at least."

"I imagined he'd be leaving to follow his own dream," she told Laurie Lee lightly.

Laurie Lee gave a little laugh. "I've made him an offer he can't refuse. And I'm prepared to make you a good offer, too, Elaine. A good salary, more than you'd make in Los Angeles, and a good place to raise children."

"I've got to get settled. Aaron will need to be enrolled in a school in a month."

"There are good schools here."

"I'd be afraid. Anthony knows they're here."

"Would you be any less afraid somewhere else? At least here you're surrounded by people who care."

Chapter Seventeen

Elaine pondered what Laurie Lee said.

"We could hire a tutor for Aaron, or even a bodyguard," Laurie Lee suggested. "If you think that best?"

Must Aaron and Amanda forever live under a cloud of fear and uncertainty? What kind of life would that be? True, she might feel easier knowing others were watching over them, but would that make their lives better? *Wasn't that trading one kind of abnormal life for another?*

It wasn't just their father she must protect them from. She didn't want them growing up feeling their security threatened.

I've got to get them away somewhere. Somewhere we can start a new life and no one knows where we are or who we are.

All this last week while everyone coped with the sadness of Emma's death she had been deciding what she must do, no matter how many arguments against the idea that Laurie Lee presented. She would bide her time until she had everything ready. She'd done that once . . . she could do it again.

"Security is one thing some children miss out on. I was fortunate in having caring foster parents." Laurie Lee was in a reminiscent mood. "Emma never got half the care and attention that every child deserves. But she overcame all of that."

"You both had foster parents? You're not really Indian, are you?"

"Hardly." Laurie Lee smiled. "My foster father used to claim he had a little Indian in him. He used to spin tales about his Indian heritage. I guess I romanticized about it. I thought up that Indian legend to promote my cosmetics. It was the very thing I needed to make my business boom."

"Your father . . . or foster father . . . raised pheasants, too, I think Emma said?"

"Right here. It was his passion." She sighed. "I only wish he could have lived to see what I've accomplished."

Previously the sheriff stopped by to talk to Mitchell.

"We're about done with our investigation," he said. "I know you think it was foul play but we've not found any evidence of that. We've determined your mother's death was accidental."

"What about Anthony Bradbury?" Mitchell's jaw tightened.

"I talked with him, and I checked his alibi with the men with whom he said he was playing poker the night in question," the sheriff answered patiently. "They confirm what he said."

"They're all lying," Elaine flared. "He was right here on these premises. We all saw him."

"Five say otherwise. I brought all this to the attention of the district attorney's office. He said unless new evidence comes to light, there's no way he can get a conviction."

Both Elaine and Laurie Lee expressed their regret after the sheriff left. They knew that Mitchell wanted to see justice done.

"I understand what you mean about power, Elaine," he said bitterly, his voice hoarse with suppressed emotion. "You'd have no chance getting custody of those children if your husband wants them. But I'm not giving up, not

when I know he killed my mother. I can't let him just walk
away. I want him punished. I'm thinking of a civil suit
against him."

After the first week Mitchell was working again, even
though he avoided the building where Emma was killed.

"He's hurting bad about his mother," Russ commented
one morning when Elaine took the children to see the latest
hatch of baby birds.

"I know." She missed her, too, as did the children.

She had been invited here by Emma, but now she must
make plans to leave. "We all miss her," she added.

"Pauline misses her, too," he said. "She's worked with
Emma for years."

"Of course, but she seemed upset even before Emma
died." She wondered if he was aware of Polly's hurt feelings. She hated standing idly by and letting a vicious person
like Veronica destroy her peace of mind.

He leaned against the board gate and gazed out across
the pheasant pen before speaking. "I guess I know what
you're saying, Elaine. I was almost certain you saw us the
day you and the kids were down by the creek. I hoped you
hadn't. I want you to know it went no farther. I wouldn't
hurt Polly for anything or anybody."

So it was Russ and Veronica who frightened her that day.
She'd been so sure it was Anthony or Martin Sills stalking
her. But since the night of Emma's death she was satisfied
that her fears were justified and not mere phantoms.

"Well, there's no fool like an old fool, they say," Russ
said wryly, and opened the gate to go in the pens.

*Especially when one person pursues another, deliber-
ately and intentionally? How could one person be so un-
caring about the effect their actions made on other lives?*
She even felt sorry for Irving, *but why did he stay with
Veronica?*

Returning to the house Pauline handed her the telephone.

"I think it's him," Polly whispered, stretching out her arm full length as though she could be contaminated if she got too close to the mouthpiece.

Elaine's heart pounded with dread. *How had he the power to do this to her? Make her shake and tremble with fear because of that power?* Still, she needed to talk to him, to know what he wanted, to determine his intentions.

"Anthony?" She tried to sound calm and unworried.

"Hello, my dear." She pictured his eyes, cold and calculating in spite of the soft cunning of his voice. "I do hope you are well?"

"What do you want?" She was not about to pretend any friendliness between them.

"I want to know when I can pick up the children?"

"Never."

"Why not keep this pleasant? I told you if you wanted a divorce, you can have it, but not the children."

"Or what? You'll kill me like you killed poor Emma?"

"I heard. That was too bad."

"Heard? You killed her that night you were here."

"I heard it was accidental."

"You heard wrong."

"If I was guilty of all you accuse me of, Elaine, I'd be a very busy man. Now, I've been thinking about schooling for Aaron. He needs to be with me so I can enroll him in the same school he attended last year. My mother is anxious about him."

"Your mother's never been anxious about anyone her whole life," she said angrily. "Anyhow, we're thinking of getting him a tutor." Elaine hoped he'd believe her even though she had made the decision to leave soon without telling anyone her true intentions.

"Really? How interesting. And who will be paying for that?" He laughed without humor.

"Laurie Lee has generously offered . . ."

This time his laugh seemed genuine. Finally he gasped, "You kill me, Elaine."

"I'd like to. Sometimes I'd really like to," she said.

"Don't force me to bring kidnapping charges against you to get what is mine." His voice was cold and threatening.

She slammed the phone down.

Needing to talk with Laurie Lee, Elaine went to her office. Before she even entered the room she saw that Laurie Lee wasn't there, but Veronica was, making a half-hearted attempt at dusting the furniture.

"I'm looking for Laurie Lee," she told Veronica.

Veronica looked up from her dusting. "Her highness didn't come to her office today." She flicked the cloth down one side of the desk and closed an open drawer.

"Is she sick?" Elaine wondered.

"Now, that's a matter of opinion." Veronica circled her head with her forefinger, and smirked.

"Veronica." Elaine was exasperated. "Maybe I'd better check with Polly."

"Why bother? Old Polly doesn't even know what's going on in this world if someone doesn't tell her. She thinks life revolves around a chicken casserole."

Elaine bit her tongue, literally, to keep from saying more. Leaving the room, she met Pauline starting up the stairs with a tray.

"Are you taking that to Laurie Lee?" she asked.

"Yes, poor dear." Pauline paused to catch her breath. "She's taking all this so hard. So pale, and she's not eating. Grieving her heart out, I'd say."

"I know."

"I'm so glad you were here. Your being here helped her a lot. She tries to hide her grief from you and Mitchell, but I'm afraid she'll make herself ill."

"Let me carry that." Elaine took the tray and followed Polly up the stairs.

Laurie Lee was sitting up in bed, looking haggard in spite of carefully applied makeup. Elaine's heart wrenched with pity, and she found herself fluttering over her much as Pauline was doing.

Laurie Lee sipped on her coffee, and broke off a bite of buttered toast. Pauline busied herself about the room before positioning herself in a chair near the bed. She held a pen poised over a pad of paper. "I need to go over those things you mentioned yesterday."

While they proceeded to discuss several tasks that needed doing and errands that needed to be run, Elaine wandered restlessly about the room, reading the awards on one wall, scrutinizing more closely the photos hanging at one side.

In the background she heard Laurie Lee dismiss several duties that Pauline brought to her attention with, "Elaine will take care of that." Or, "Tell Elaine to use her own judgment on that one." Once she said, "Tell Veronica I said to see to it."

She's depending on me, but I can't help that. I have to go away without her knowing. She moved restlessly about the room, pausing by two matching chairs covered in blue velvet to gaze closely at a painting hanging above them. Surrounded by other smaller paintings was the one she painted of Aaron that Emma chose from her collection a few months after she married Anthony.

Until she saw it again she'd forgotten all about it. Aaron was much younger then. Probably about four. *Had Emma given it to Laurie Lee instead of keeping it for herself?*

She waited until Pauline went back downstairs before mentioning it.

"That painting of Aaron . . . where did you get it?"

Laurie Lee's eyes went immediately to the painting.

"Why, Emma gave it to me for a gift. Is that Aaron?"

"Of course it's Aaron. Didn't she tell you?"

"She might have." Laurie Lee scowled. "I've had it for years."

"I thought she wanted it for herself."

"Sounds like Emma, doesn't it? She knows I love paintings of children." She yawned elaborately, dismissing the whole subject.

Mitchell knocked at the open door. "May I come in?"

"Of course, Mitch." Laurie Lee lifted the tray from her knees, indicating that Elaine was to remove it. "I want to talk to you, too. We need to discuss some ideas I have for expanding the pheasant business."

He frowned. "Can't that wait? There's something else I need to go over with you."

"What is it?" Laurie Lee motioned for him to sit in the chair next to her bed that Pauline had vacated.

"I must go see about the children," Elaine said tactfully, moving away.

"Can you wait, Elaine? Russ is watching them. I want to talk about my mother, and I'd like your opinion on something."

Elaine set the tray down on a table and waited.

"I intend to make an appointment to see a lawyer about pressing charges in a civil suit against Bradford. Who is your lawyer, Laurie Lee?"

"Malcolm and Malcolm. But they're corporate lawyers. Not criminal. Still, they might talk to you . . . give you some advice." She looked him directly in the eyes. "Are you sure you want to do this?"

"I certainly do. If that man thinks he can get by with murder . . ."

"There might be quite a controversy," she warned.

"I'm sorry. I know you hate any kind of adverse publicity, but I must do what I think is right."

"We must get a guard to be with the children all the time, then."

"I think the contrary. I think when he sees we'll fight, he'll back off."

Laurie Lee looked grim. "I just hope you're right," she said.

It would take more than the threat of charges against him to stop Anthony, Elaine thought.

Chapter Eighteen

Elaine worried all day about the aftermath if Mitchell carried out his plan to bring charges against Anthony. She really didn't blame him for wanting to see his mother's killer punished, no matter how difficult that might make things for all of them if he did.

Any action he took would be apt to cause trouble. Anthony believed in fighting dirty. When crossed, he always expected to exact revenge. *Who better to retaliate against than herself and the children?* He would act when and where she least expected. She would never draw a free breath, never walk down a street without looking back over one shoulder in concern for Amanda and Aaron . . . and for herself.

Aaron had to be enrolled in school. She must reach some sort of decision and forget about letting Laurie Lee make plans for the children, no matter how tempting it sounded.

If she stayed here, like Laurie Lee suggested, and Anthony managed to get Aaron or Amanda . . . or both . . . away from her, she would never be able to forgive herself. With the threat of Anthony hanging over their heads, everything they did, every place they went, anything they wanted to do in the future would need to be weighed. Their guard must not be let down even for one instant. Birthday parties, trips to town, picnics in the park, simple things that children loved to do, would never be simple.

If they stayed how could any of them here really protect them? How could she sleep freely at night, aware that any hour of every day must be viewed with misgivings, with waiting for something to happen?

And who had protected Emma?

When she came here she knew that life from then on would be difficult, but she hadn't thought it would include murder.

Mitchell and Laurie Lee and even Pauline would try to talk her out of leaving if they knew. If she was going to gamble the children's welfare she must keep secret when she was leaving and where she was going. Not to Los Angeles, that much she knew, Anthony was sure to think of that.

She set a certain time to act. *Friday . . . at midnight.* Using the same procedure she'd used when she fled Chicago, she carried out extra clothing, and even put her cell phone in the pocket of the jacket she intended wearing when she left, although she wasn't sure she would be safe using it.

Each morning she insisted the children wear a sweater or an extra garment when they went out to play on the pretext that it was cool outdoors. Once outside, she would encourage them to remove the extra items which she would secret away.

Within a few days she had accumulated quite a bundle of clothing in the trunk of her car along with other small possessions she didn't want to leave behind.

Sometimes, worrying about the outcome of her plans, she became almost sick with fear of the unknown . . . alone. Even if Mitchell hadn't decided to bring charges against Anthony, if the three of them remained in this vicinity, their lives would never quite be their own. The children's safety rested on her ability to sneak away from Laurie Lee's without anyone learning of her intent.

Friday came.

The children made their usual trip to the pheasant pens that morning, but they never realized it was their last visit to see the birds. Later they took a dip in the pool.

She watched them splashing about. This is the way their life should be, she thought. Days filled with fun.

After lunch she carried out her easel and the case of paints and brushes, and painted them while they admired the pheasants. On the way back to the house, while they ran ahead, she stopped at her car to deposit her painting paraphernalia in the back.

Friday evening she felt a sense of sadness when they sat down in the family dining room for their evening meal. This would be the last time she would be eating here, at this table, with these people. She might never see any of them again for if any of them knew her future whereabouts, then Anthony, using any and every means possible, would find out.

She would have preferred to confide her plans to Laurie Lee or Mitchell, to thank Laurie Lee for all she'd done, and not sever her ties to Mitchell. She rehearsed her plans in her mind. She would drive to some distant city and sell her car. She would buy cheap luggage and take the children to a bus station where they would leave for another city, maybe one farther south.

What type of work she might find was the big question in her mind. A safe place to live. A good environment for the children. Those desires were now uppermost in her list of requirements. She remembered how important it once seemed to ride in a limo, to dine in fancy restaurants, to buy the best of clothing. Now all of that seemed insignificant.

She had enough money left to tide her over for a bit.

That was critical—the children must not do without. There was much to be worked out. But she would manage. Somehow. She had to. For all their sakes.

She tucked the children into bed at their customary hour, and made herself sit with Laurie Lee and Mitchell, watching a television show. No one followed the gag lines of a comedy. Elaine was sure that both Laurie Lee's and Mitchell's minds were on Emma, as was hers.

She pretended to be interested in the musical that Laurie Lee switched to, but now that the night had arrived for her departure, she wanted to be gone.

Mitchell yawned elaborately several times before he got up, saying, he was heading off to bed. She chatted about inconsequential things with Laurie Lee for a few minutes, before declaring that she was tired and was going to bed, too.

After showering, she dressed in dark slacks and a sweater and climbed into bed, fully clothed except for her shoes. She didn't try to sleep, but lay awake listening to night sounds. The house quieted. She made herself wait until the clock hands pointed exactly to twelve before slipping out of bed to place a note, previously written, on her dresser top.

In the note she apologized to both Laurie Lee and to Mitchell, briefly explaining why she felt such secrecy necessary. She made no promise to get in touch.

While Amanda slept she dressed her in jeans and a long sleeve shirt and put on her socks and the pink tennis shoes she loved. She murmured in her sleep, annoyed at being disturbed, but never opened her eyes.

She left her on her cot while she went into the next room to awaken Aaron. He sat up in bed the minute she touched him, rubbing his eyes, and saying, "What's the matter, Laine?"

"Sh-h-h," she whispered, and placed a finger on his lips. "We're leaving. I don't want anyone to hear us."

"Why? Where we going?" He was wide awake now.

"We're not safe from your father here. Get dressed." She handed him his shirt and pants which he pulled on over his shortie pajamas.

She was certain she could count on Aaron to be quiet as they slipped out of the house, but Amanda could not be trusted to not say something, to not cry out.

She bent over the little girl, gathering her up in her arms. "Amanda," she whispered directly in her ear, "be very quiet. Do you understand? We're leaving, so don't say one word after we go out the door. Understand?"

"Why?" Amanda whined, still half asleep.

"Because someone might try to stop us. I'm going to open the door now, so don't make a sound."

Amanda wasn't ready yet to be quiet.

"Who dressed me?" she demanded.

"I did. Now, are you going to be quiet, or not?"

"Okay." She was vexed as well as puzzled.

"Promise."

"I promise," she giggled sleepily, enjoying this new game.

"Sh-h-h." Elaine pulled on her jacket before opening the door to the hall.

Anthony had gloated when he said that some of her friends were his friends, but who was he specifically talking about?

Carrying Amanda, and followed by a trembling Aaron, they started down the hallway. She led the way down the back stairs, going slowly, quietly. Any minute she expected someone to call to her, to stop her, wanting to know where she was going at this time of night.

At the back door she hesitated, listening. Their combined breathing sounded loud in her ears. She eased back the dead bolt. As she turned the knob to go out she heard a thud behind her, but she never stopped to check it out.

A glance at Amanda's face as they passed under the yard

light showed her that her small daughter's eyes were dancing in delight at this silent trek out in the dark of the night.
Another giggle was welling up in her throat and she placed
one hand over Amanda's mouth. The laugh rumbled away
inside the small chest.

Neither child said a word as they reached the car. Elaine
opened the door on the driver's side and the children
slipped into the back.

Amanda was wide awake now. Aaron kept watching out
the window as though he suspected someone to arrive on
the scene to prevent their leaving.

"Fasten your seat belt, Aaron," she said quietly, leaning
over to snap Amanda into her car seat.

She got in, turned the key in the switch. The engine
throbbed. She eased the vehicle forward down the drive
without turning on the lights.

She could see easily. The drive was a gray streak between rows of dark bushes that grew along each side. She
glanced back at the house and up at the windows that
opened off the back stair landing. There was a movement
so slight that she wondered if she'd actually seen one. *Or
had there been a breeze that lifted the drapery, fluttering.
Or had someone stood there watching, silent and unpro-
testing, while she and the children sneaked across the yard
and left in the car?*

Chapter Nineteen

The children, tired and trusting, were quiet as they drove through the night. Amanda's eyes closed even before they reached Fulton Falls, and Aaron was becoming drowsy.

Elaine kept a watchful eye on the speedometer as she drove along the dark and deserted streets of the sleeping town. She had no desire to be stopped by the police or a patrolman. Now and then she caught glimpses of the bright neon lights of a bar, still open, or an all night laundry, but having seen the town only when it was bustling with activity, there was an almost eerie feeling at seeing no one around.

After passing the city limits sign leading out of town she pressed her foot down on the gas pedal, anxious to put miles between her and the place where she last saw Anthony.

What lay ahead? She prayed she was doing the right thing and that no harm would come to any of them.

Several miles down the highway she caught the lights of a car in her rearview mirror. She watched. When she slowed, it slowed, never trying to pass her, or turn off at a crossroad. She told herself that Anthony couldn't be following her. There was no way he could know that she was out here on the road. She sped up, going too fast down the two lane highway. The other car sped up, too, but still not passing. This was no chance occurrence. This was planned, a dire scheme worked out.

She remembered the movement she'd seen in the window back at Laurie Lee's house. Had someone been watching her, someone at Laurie Lee's who notified another person? Was that person the driver of the other car? Was it Anthony? Had he been staying in Fulton Falls all this time?

"Some of your friends, are my friends," Anthony had boasted. *Had that friend been a member of Laurie Lee's household? And for what reason would he have tipped off Anthony? Who was it . . . Veronica? Irving?*

The car behind her moved closer until his front bumper was almost touching Elaine's bumper. If she stopped suddenly he would run into her car, and maybe hurt the children.

"Laine," Aaron cried. "He's gonna wreck us."

Elaine saw the turnoff ahead to a wayside park.

"Sit down and hang on," she told Aaron.

When her car was almost upon the turnoff, she pressed down on the accelerator and gained a few feet of space between her and the other car. Giving her pursuer no chance to anticipate her actions, she turned her car sharply into the drive, did a complete circle, and was heading back out and down the opposite direction of the highway before the driver of the long black car could stop.

She made no pretense of controlling her speed as she entered Fulton Falls again. She raced along, her free hand plunging in her jacket pocket for her cell phone, but her pocket was empty. Memory stirred. She remembered the thud when she pulled on her jacket while still in her room. Her phone had evidently fallen from her pocket then.

She raced down Main Street but no one showed even when she ran a red light.

She saw that the other car had come up behind her again, keeping his distance, yet so near that she was unable to draw away from him, to lose him as she sped along.

Besides, Anthony would guess that I'm heading back to Laurie Lee's, she thought wildly. *He wouldn't have to keep that close to her.*

"Let's go back, Laine," Aaron shouted from the back seat. "Let's go back."

She was concentrating too intently on the road to assure him that she was trying desperately to do just that.

She told herself that she was handling the car well enough, but there must still be a mile to go. *Could she make it back to Laurie Lee's and safety?*

When the other driver pulled alongside of her, she wondered if that was a ploy to block her from turning off the road again.

"Stop, Laine," Aaron yelled.

She knew she shouldn't return, but she was afraid to stop fearing what would happen to the three of them if she did stop. She had to keep her foot on the gas pedal—she had to reach the farm. There was no way she could compete in a hand to hand struggle if he should force her out of the car and make off with the children.

The road to the farm angled sharply ahead to the right. Far up the tree-lined lane Laurie Lee's house loomed, a dark hulk against a lighter sky, a house that guaranteed safety for the children and for herself.

She knew she should slow down to make the turn, and she prayed without realizing that she was praying. She swung the car hard to the right without braking. She didn't turn sharp enough and her continued speed carried her too far. Her car came to an abrupt and jarring halt with the front wheels lodged in the ditch.

The impact threw her forward, her hands still clenching the steering wheel. She twisted around in the seat to check on Aaron, who was terrified but unhurt in the security of his seat belt, but Amanda was crying angrily at the rough treatment she'd had.

Regaining her senses Elaine got out of the car. Looking around for the other vehicle she discovered it had plunged into a ditch on the opposite side of the road. The occupant was climbing out, swaying a little, and talking on a cell phone taken from his pocket. She peered for an instant through the darkness, trying to decide if it was Anthony, but the person wore clothing that was as dark as the night, and she couldn't be sure. *Who was he calling? The person who notified him of her departure?*

She reached in and released Amanda from her seat. Aaron had already freed himself and was running up the lane, reaching the driveway ahead of her. He was hollering aloud, first, "Laurie Lee," and then "Mitchell." Surely someone would hear him and come to their rescue.

Running with Amanda in her arms, Elaine was acutely aware of heavy footfalls thudding behind her. Even their breathing was loud to her ears, and came above the sound of her own labored breath. Amanda had quit hollering, burying her face on her mother's shoulder. Not looking up, not hanging on, but a dead weight that left Elaine uncertain as to how much longer she could carry the load.

She tried standing Amanda down, hoping to make better time if Amanda could run along beside her, but Amanda seemed to be merely hopping up and down on her short little legs, not making any progress. She stumbled and fell. Elaine, winded and gasping, dragged her up into her aching arms once more.

She glanced back and saw that her pursuer still followed, although the distance between them was greater than it had been, and he was limping rather badly. Evidently he had hurt a leg when his car plunged into the ditch.

In spite of the apparent pain he seemed to have caught his second wind and was once again closing the gap between them, gaining a bit of ground every step of the way.

She never considered that she was running exactly where he wanted her to run, never dreamed that she was playing right into his scheme as she ran across the yard and started up the walk to the front door. Her arms ached from the weight of the child, and a searing pain throbbed in her chest.

Aaron reached the steps leading into the house ahead of her. An outside light by the entry flashed on, illuminating the entire area. A sob of relief tore from her throat as she got ready to make the last mad dash to safety.

Aaron let out a cry as someone opened the front door and stepped out, grabbing him by the arm and clamping a cloth over his mouth, smothering his scream.

Her legs trembled, weak and useless. She sank to the top step, Amanda at her side, unable to hold onto her a minute longer, not even protesting except for a feeble wave of one hand at the person who was pressing a foul smelling rag over her face, choking off what little breath she had left.

Amanda, silent, fear filling her eyes, pushed against her mother. Elaine clung to the fragile arms, the tiny hands, but everything was fading away and a great roar filled her ears. She heard Amanda cry, but the sound seemed to be coming from some distant place, echoing as though through a tunnel, sounding vacant and hollow.

Her grip on the child loosened and she felt Amanda being lifted out of her arms, felt the hard step under her head, heard Amanda's crying stop, and then, darkly, nothing at all.

The last conscious thought she had faded away, fuzzy and uncertain: *Why was Irving treating Aaron like that?*

Chapter Twenty

*W*as she dreaming? Or was this real, this feeling of being dragged over hard, rough ground, of being lifted and dropped unceremoniously onto a seat. She wanted to complain, but she was too tired. When she heard the start of an engine she knew that she was in a motor vehicle, that the softness under her head was the cushioned seat of a car. Even her eyelids felt weighted down though she struggled to open them. A gentle sensation of movement quieted her inner turmoil, the steady throb of the engine comforting her much as she once comforted Amanda when she was a baby by taking her for rides.

In spite of her desire to know that Amanda and Aaron were safe, her mind was too confused, her thoughts too jumbled to speak. She formed the words in her mind but she couldn't get them past her lips. She couldn't say what she wanted to say.

She hadn't even been able to protest when muscular hands had lifted her into the car, but now, awakened by her inert body being tugged at again she tried to tell whoever lifted her to leave her alone, but she sensed she wasn't saying whole words, that only meaningless muttering escaped her lips.

Had hours elapsed since she first entered that endless tunnel of darkness, or had it been a lifetime?

Fresh air hit her in the face, and she flung out her hands, fumbling, grasping at nothing. She caught a glimpse of dawn breaking across the eastern sky, streaks of gold reflecting against low clouds, edging them in salmon pink. She thought it the loveliest sight she'd ever seen.

Birds fluttered in and out of overhead trees, roused by dawn and by the unusual disturbance on the ground directly beneath them. She wanted to see who had hold of her shoulders, dragging her, but she hadn't strength enough to make the effort to look. Someone shoved her up on her feet against a solid wall, her back against wood siding while a door was being opened. Her ankles wobbled and her stomach heaved. She could feel herself slipping to her knees.

"Watch she don't fall," someone growled in a low voice. There was only a grunted reply.

Where was she? A musty odor filled her nostrils. She was in an enclosure somewhere, and regrettably, she could no longer see the beauty of the dawn. She tried to speak, but she knew her words made no sense even to herself for she only said, "It's very pretty."

"It's the anesthesia," one of her captors said. "She's talking nonsense."

She wanted to say, "No, it's the beautiful sky." It seemed very important her.

Someone half walked, half pulled her across a room, and dropped her none too gently onto something soft. A door closed. Footsteps faded away.

Time passed, yet stood still. How long she slept she had no idea. When she awoke, she lay absolutely quiet with only her eyes moving as she tried to decide where she was, almost afraid to look for fear of what she might see.

Finally she sat upright. The room where she was being held was small and dingy. Spiderwebs hung in every corner. She shuddered, ready to feel revulsion at what had been her bed, but, though the floor was dirty, a clean blanket had been spread out for her to lie on.

Her heart flip-flopped in wonder and delight at the sight of Amanda and Aaron curled up together in a far corner of the room, both sleeping, a big soft blanket spread out beneath them and another covering them.

She struggled to her feet, dizzy, swaying, one hand against the wall for support, willing herself along to the pallet where they lay.

"Oh, Amanda. Aaron." She dropped down beside them, overjoyed to see them, checking that their breathing seemed regular and natural. She had no desire to wake them.

She got to her feet more easily this time, and made her way to the board door. She turned the knob, and gave it a hard yank, but it was locked on the outside.

Daylight came through a single window square, with cross pieces forming four separate small panes. She staggered over to peer out. The square of light was filled with a mat of thick webs.

She looked around for something to use to brush them away. An old dresser stood against a wall, the upper drawer sagging open. From it she took a dirty rag and wiped the glass fairly clean, allowing her to press her face closer to the pane.

Weeds grew in front of the window, but through the gaps between stems and leaves she made out a mass of pine trees. In the distance smoky blue hills melded into a far away sky.

She had hoped to open the window and escape with the children, but looking closer she saw that nails had been pounded in at the sash, preventing it from being raised.

If she broke it out, would someone hear? Or would only her captors hear? Was anyone else even around? Had she and the children been locked in here and deserted? There was no movement or sound to indicate the presence of anyone nearby.

Turning her gaze as far to the right as she could she barely made out the outline of a shed or a lean-to or maybe an attachment to the place where she and the children were locked in. Across the yard was a rock wall, with weeds growing up between rocks that had fallen away.

She turned away, intending to try the door again, but before she could twist the knob, there was a scratching outside, and suddenly the weathered board door swung inward.

She gasped, drawing back in surprise. Anthony stood there, smiling, but the smile never reached his eyes. He was shaven and neat and he carried a box of food.

"Hungry?" he asked.

"Hardly." She stepped farther back into the room as he indicated she should do.

Leaving the door hang open he placed the box on the dresser top. She contemplated the open doorway that suggested freedom, but as he withdrew to the entrance again, the smirk on his face told her that he realized she would never run without the children.

"What are we doing here in this godforsaken place?" she demanded.

He laughed. He could always laugh at something that amused him, and it was amusing as long as it didn't affect him.

"My dear," he said, his voice heavy with ridicule, "I thought this might be a nice home for you. It will be all you can afford when I'm done with you."

"What do you mean?" She tried to appear unconcerned, to not let him see her fear.

"My lawyers are working on the papers. Should be ready tomorrow. Irving will bring them out."

"Irving? Papers?"

"Giving me full and complete custody of Amanda. Of course Aaron is not your responsibility at all. If you sign them, agree not to harass me nor contest the agreement, I'll agree not to press kidnapping charges against you for taking my son away."

"Never."

"Never is a long time. If you don't, I'll take Amanda and Aaron away and you'll never see either of them again."

"No." She shook her head. "Take me to court if you want Amanda. I won't give her to you, ever."

He looked at her with contempt. "Don't be ridiculous. You kidnapped them. I'd win full custody. You're ridiculous. You never did use your brain."

He left her as suddenly as he came, pulling the door shut behind him. She heard him wiring the door shut again.

The children sat up, mystified.

"What are we doing here?" Aaron implored.

Amanda batted heavy-lidded eyes. "I don't like it."

She tried to console them, but there was no way she could explain away something like this. She knew she must tell them the truth. Yet she wasn't sure what to do.

"Your father is holding us here until he gets some papers he wants me to sign. He won't hurt us. You needn't be afraid."

Strangely enough, she believed those words. Anthony had no reason to hurt them. They were back under his control. All she could do was comfort the children and assure them that all would be well. Though she doubted that Anthony would physically harm them at this point, she had no doubt that if he decided to do so, he could spirit the children away as he threatened, and she'd never see either of them again. He would brainwash Aaron into believing that he hadn't seen what his son was so certain he'd witnessed, and convince Amanda that her mother never loved her.

She opened the box and for the children's benefit, she exclaimed over the contents. There were sandwiches, bright red apples, a thermos of coffee, a jug of chocolate milk, and several individual boxes of raisins.

"Just like a picnic," she crowed.

"I've got to go potty." Amanda placed her sandwich carefully on her napkin.

"Me, too." Aaron squeezed his legs together.

She went over to the door and pounded on it.

Anthony opened it almost immediately.

"The children and I need to go to the bathroom," she said stiffly, and motioned toward the children who waited in the middle of the room, staring wide-eyed at their father.

"Hm-m-m." Anthony regarded them with deliberate calculation. "This is a primitive neighborhood, however, we've considered this possibility, and sort of dusted out the small building for this very likelihood. You may all go . . ." He eyed them with amusement. "One at a time, of course."

"Let Amanda go alone? To an outdoor privy? There could be snakes or . . . or . . ." Elaine's anger was unrestrained.

He held up one hand. "I've already checked it out. It's safe. Come Amanda." He reached for her hand.

Amanda regarded him thoughtfully, rubbing her chin against her shoulder, but necessity overcame her reluctance. She placed her small hand in his and walked out of the building through tall weeds. The door was fastened again from the outside, but Elaine stood at the dirty window and watched their progress for as long as she could see them.

One by one he escorted them to the small ramshackle building, each time locking in those remaining behind.

The hours passed slowly. Elaine invented games to keep the children entertained, and waited in silent anxiety each time they needed to go to the outhouse for fear he might whisk them away the minute one or the other was out of sight.

From the glimpses of the surrounding area that she memorized each time she was escorted to the toilet, she couldn't even hazard a guess as to their whereabouts. That it was in a remote area was her only conclusion for she saw no telephone lines, no visible farm buildings or cattle or other livestock.

"Where are we?" she asked Anthony on her second trip out.

He just shook his head at her and declined to answer.

"How long must we stay here?"

"As soon as Irving gets here, you can sign the papers and be on your way immediately. No one ever comes here, so no use hoping for that."

"You mean no unforeseen passerby will pop in and wonder what's going on? Is this your place? Your hideaway?"

His laugh held no humor. "Irving lived here as a boy. I doubt anyone has lived here since."

"Why is Irving helping you? How do you know him?"

"Questions. Questions. Irving isn't the only one. So many people have a need for money."

"And money is power, isn't it?" Her voice lost the belligerent tone as she asked softly, "Anthony, please say you won't take the children from me." She hoped to appeal to his better side, if there was one.

"You took them from me," he reminded her, his lips squeezed tightly together.

"They need me. They need to be with me."

"Children get over almost everything." He walked behind her on their way back to the cabin.

By afternoon keeping the children contented was becoming more and more impossible. They had investigated each corner of the room, were repulsed by the dirt, shrank from the spiders, their clothing dirty with clinging bits of webs. Digging into a drawer to see what they could find, something stirred and leaped out at them, scurrying across the floor.

Elaine shrieked and jumped back.

The door opened and Anthony looked in at her. She stared at him, one hand clawing at her throat, her heart pounding.

"What's the matter?" His look was suspicious.

"A mouse," she gasped. "I . . . I . . ."

He tipped his head backward, laughed aloud, and went out again, closing the door behind him. Angrily, she saw that Aaron, too, was doubled over in laughter, while Amanda, appearing puzzled, was uncertain whether to laugh or cry.

Her irritation at Aaron was unjustified, yet how dare he look and act like his father?

Night fell. Anthony brought them another box of food and gave her an unfeeling apology.

"I'm afraid you must spend another night here, my dear." His voice held no real emotion. "Irving hasn't got back yet."

"He's probably got smart and changed his mind. He's probably decided not to get mixed up in a kidnapping."

"I can hardly be charged with kidnapping my own children."

"How about me? You're holding me against my will. I'll testify to that."

He walked over to the door, flung it wide open and took a step away.

"No, I'm not. Go if you want to."

She reached down for the children.

"I said *you*." He blocked her path. "The children stay. They're mine. More mine than yours. Are you going?"

"Without them? Never." Defiant, she dropped down on the blanket again, pulling the box of food toward her. He threw her a look of disdain as he went out the door.

She wasn't hungry, but the children ate greedily. They went to sleep soon after. There was nothing else for them to do, she supposed. Bored, she picked up the thermos and poured out a cup of steaming coffee. The aroma wafted upward. She peered into the cup appreciatively. There was a powdery substance floating on the surface of the liquid.

Of course. How else could the children sleep so long?

She poured the contents out on the floor. Their jug of chocolate milk had probably disguised any chalky flavor, but it was too late now to prevent their drinking it.

She got up and walked to the door and back, to the window and back and to the window again. A dim light shone through the dirty pane. Soft rays fell across the floor from a far away moon, touching the sleeping children on the pad where they lay. She was awake, alert, thankful that she'd not touched her coffee.

Muffled voices came from beyond the closed door. She recognized Anthony's soft voice, but who was he talking to? Pressing her eye against a crack between two boards, she tried to see who was outside, but the night was too dark, the yard shadowed by too many tall trees. Continuing to squint through the narrow space she tried to turn her gaze in the direction of the voices. A dark hulk moved in between her and the light of a fluorescent lantern carried by Anthony. She couldn't see the person to whom he was talking, but she supposed that Irving must be back.

Anthony set the lantern down. His voice rose, softly insinuating, persuasive, his arms waving over his head. "Now this is entirely unnecessary, my dear."

"The entire matter was unnecessary," came a voice barely audible to Elaine. "Now, bring Andrew and Amanda and Elaine out of that filthy hovel."

"You mean Aaron?"

"Call him what you choose. He's Andrew to me."

Elaine felt a thrill of relief when she recognized the other voice. Only one person's voice had that husky tone, that certain quality.

Laurie Lee. Laurie Lee had come to save them.

Chapter Twenty-one

"What's troubling you? This matter is no concern of yours." Anthony's voice remained smooth and unruffled. "You made your choice a long time ago."

"Choice? I had a choice? Holding the threat of what I did as a child over my head made it seem like I didn't have one. What could I do? You were determined to never let me see Andrew, no matter what dirty tactics you used against me."

"Well, one must work with what one has. I'm sure if the law had even questioned you there would have been some real juicy headlines. The media would have had a heyday without any help from me."

Silence followed. Elaine pressed closer to the door. *What on earth were they talking about?*

"You know," Anthony was speaking again, his voice coming clearly through the still night, "you really shouldn't have told me all that stuff when we got married. I wasn't a priest to grant absolution. You should have been smart enough to keep quiet."

Laurie Lee and Anthony were married?

"I thought I owed you that . . . that I was supposed to tell you about my life . . . that married people trusted each other enough to confess their past, especially what they did as children. But you used my confession as a threat to have your own way when we divorced. And don't tell me you really wanted Andrew. You just wanted to get even with me. I couldn't let Andrew grow up believing his mother killed someone."

Elaine couldn't believe what she was hearing. *Aaron's real name was Andrew? Laurie Lee his mother? And he didn't know?*

"Someone? Your father. Why don't you say it? And why don't you admit that the real reason you didn't want the media to find out was the worry about what it would do to your business? You would have been ruined. It wasn't just Aaron that you wanted to protect."

"My father tried to kill me and Buddy. When he came back to make certain I hadn't got out of that well, I had to do something. I was only eleven." Her voice was anguished.

"So you hit him with a rock and pushed him in. What will your business associates and friends think when they read about the real you? You'll be front page, I promise that."

"And you'll make certain the media gets every gruesome detail, won't you?"

"Of course. You're not keeping up your end of our agreement."

"I don't believe you're in any position to argue." Elaine watched as Laurie Lee opened her handbag and took out something before letting the bag fall to her feet. At first Elaine couldn't make out what she held, but when Laurie Lee said, "Now, who's in charge?" she decided she had to be holding a gun and evidently had it pointed at Anthony.

There was instant quiet. Through the crack Elaine saw Anthony move a step to his right, nearer to Laurie Lee.

"Laurie Lee, don't be stupid," Anthony commanded sternly. "Put that thing away." He took another step in the same direction.

"Don't try anything," Laurie Lee warned. She, too, took a step to her right, keeping the distance between them the same. "Get Elaine and the children out of there and we'll be on our way. When I figured out where you were heading I called Mitchell on my cell phone. I'd been watching Irving earlier. When his car pulled out I asked Veronica what he was up to. At first she said she didn't know, but when I threatened to send her and Irving packing, she said he'd said something about going back to his birthplace. So I started out for this god-awful place."

"I'm surprised you found it even then." Elaine saw what Anthony was up to. By keeping Laurie Lee involved in conversation, he was gradually working himself closer to her. "I couldn't have found it without Irving," Anthony said dryly. "Even if you take Aaron now, I won't let you keep him."

"Why? You don't want him. Emma told me how you treated him."

"He's had every luxury . . ."

"With that cold fish you call mother? No one to really love him?" She broke into a sob. "Give up custody and I'll give you controlling interest in my business."

"Don't be ridiculous. I have more money than I can ever use. Someone else tried to persuade me with that same argument." His voice took on a sarcastic tone.

"I know. I know."

"Emma. Your very best friend. Anything to keep you from being hurt. That's all she cared about."

"I know," she said again. "You even convinced her to help you even though she knew what it meant to me to finally have Andrew under my roof again after I realized who he really was. But you used her desire to protect me at any cost to help you to get him in your custody, didn't you? She thought it was for my own good."

"Sills convinced her of that when he came across her in a clothing store." Anthony sounded triumphant. "Sills finally persuaded her to help me get Aaron by convincing her it would save you from all the bad publicity."

"She should have known that Andrew was all that really mattered. She knew how tormented I was . . . letting him stay with you to keep my past a secret."

"Is that why you killed her?" Anthony took another step to his right.

Elaine gasped, horrified at what she was seeing and hearing. *It was too unbelievable What was he accusing Laurie Lee of doing? And why wasn't she denying his accusation? How could anyone kill their best friend?*

"That night of the Pow-Wow I was so angry when I found out that Emma was actually helping you get your hands on him. She never denied it. She presumed to know what was best for me." A sob caught in her throat. "I'd have kept Elaine and Amanda with me forever just to be close to Andrew."

"You should never have invited them into your house."

"I didn't. Emma did. Have you hurt them?"

"They're out, if you know what I mean. They're asleep, but okay." He took another step to the right, closing the gap between them even more.

"Drugged. I know you."

"I guess it's not so hard to take matters into your own hands after you've killed someone once."

"My father . . . in self-defense."

"No, I mean Martin Sills."

Again Laurie Lee didn't deny his accusation.

"Martin." She uttered his name with complete disgust. "While waiting for the others at the Circle Inn I saw that he was getting ready to pick up Andrew where she hid him.

She'd ducked into the dining room, supposedly to check on tables. At that time I didn't know she was working *with* you. I really thought that she was trying to protect Andrew."

Laurie Lee seemed suddenly aware that she was heading in the direction Anthony wanted her to go. As Elaine watched through the crack she knew Laurie Lee was insane. Laurie Lee stopped and took a step back, coming to a standstill directly in front of the cabin door.

Elaine was horrified to see that Irving was hiding among overgrown bushes near the corner of the building. He stood motionless, blending into the leafy branches in the dark. Elaine was convinced he was waiting for Laurie Lee to get close enough so he could grab the gun away from her. But from everything that had happened, she wasn't sure of anything.

Elaine wondered if she should holler at Laurie Lee, warn her? *But if she did, wouldn't that make the two men aware that she was not drugged? How then could she help the children? And how could she trust her own judgment—she had made so many mistakes.*

Anthony got Laurie Lee's attention again. "You'd confided to Emma your sordid past, and why you must avoid the media investigating your life. She knew what they would do to you."

"I was a child."

"Even so . . . you'd have been destroyed." Anthony took a step to his right, and she to hers. "You and your brother."

Now that Laurie Lee was nearer, her voice was clearly audible.

"I thought at first my father had killed Buddy until he came and pulled me out when Father went looking for him."

"Your brother is here," Irving said, springing out of the shadows. His arms went around her from behind, pinning her arms to her sides. He grabbed the gun out of her hand and tossed it to Anthony.

"Buddy."

"Sorry, dear *cousin*. Or can I call you 'sister' now?"

"Sister? When you're working with him after all I've done for you?"

"A hired servant, me and my wife both, while you live in luxury?"

"That's what your wife has convinced you to think? She's nothing but . . ."

"Don't say it, Laurie Lee." His voice was low and threatening.

"Why, then? Is Anthony giving you more money?"

"Emma convinced me the night of the Pow-Wow that sending Aaron back to his father would be best for everyone. So when I contacted Anthony, he promised to set me and Veronica up for life. Veronica's been wanting to go to Florida. Now we can."

"I knew she had a hand in this. Why are you letting her ruin your life?" Laurie Lee's voice shook with emotion.

"Enough talk," Anthony interrupted. He motioned for Laurie Lee to back away. "Did you get the papers, Irving?"

"Got 'em right here."

"Okay. You take the children and start back to Chicago," Anthony instructed. "I'll stay here until the drug wears off so Elaine can sign the papers."

"Take both of them?"

"On second thought, leave Amanda for now. That will give me additional leverage with Elaine. But I expect that when she sees that Aaron is gone she'll be no trouble at all."

The sound of someone unlocking the door sent Elaine scampering to her blanket. She dropped down and closed her eyes, feigning sleep.

The knob rattled. The door opened.

"She won't wake up?" Irving sounded apprehensive.

"I put enough drops in her coffee to keep her sleeping for hours," came Anthony's voice from outside. "She'll sleep all night."

Elaine lay quiet as she heard someone enter the room, heard a grunt of exertion as a drugged Aaron was lifted up off the floor, heard footsteps receding, and the door close. Irving's arms were full with Aaron and he didn't wire the door shut on the outside as he left. He probably presumed that she was out and would remain that way for awhile.

If only she could do something to let Laurie Lee know that she was awake and ready to help.

She stood at the door looking out through the crack again. While Anthony and Irving were busy with opening Anthony's car and getting Aaron settled on the back seat, Laurie Lee skirted across the weedy yard. Elaine guessed that her intent was to come up from the other side and try to stop them from leaving.

Dare she pick up Amanda and flee into the dense woods that she couldn't even see through in the daytime? Should she expect Laurie Lee to help her no matter what she'd confessed to? Could she trust her?

There had to be some sort of road or trail, or how would they have got here? She should chance it, she decided. Anywhere was better for Amanda to be than with her father.

But first, was there any way she might help Aaron?

She moved quickly across the dirty, gritty floor toward the outside door. On various trips to the toilet she gave her surroundings special attention. She knew there was a rusty, wire fence hanging loose at one side. And she'd spied a dilapidated car without tires, the doors hanging open and the hood up. Weeds, growing head high, were even protruding through a broken window of the car, and around a rock wall that was in the corner of the yard next to it.

She opened the door of the room she'd been kept in and stepped out. No one noticed. No one stopped her. Through the thicket of trees she caught a flash of light. *Could that be the lights of a car? Someone Anthony called earlier? Veronica coming to join her husband? Or maybe Mitchell? Or had Laurie Lee lied to Anthony when she said she called Mitchell to tell him where they were heading?*

She kept in the shadows as best she could as she made her way around behind the hut where Amanda still lay sleeping. Anthony's car was parked behind pine trees. Irving stood by the driver's door getting last minute instructions from Anthony.

Anthony was winning after all.

She watched Laurie Lee again and wondered if she had a plan. She was skirting the yard, thrusting the weeds aside as she approached Anthony's car.

"Laurie Lee," Elaine called softly. Her only chance lay in surprising Anthony, in keeping him from knowing that she was no longer drugged.

Laurie Lee must not have heard her for she was coming around on the other side of the car, closer than Elaine.

What would Aaron think, how would he feel when he awoke and found himself back under his father's jurisdiction? He would think he'd been abandoned. She couldn't let that happen.

She pushed her way through the undergrowth, trying to follow the path she'd seen Laurie Lee take. Dark clouds scudded across the sky, and in between the clouds, the stars shone, white and cold. Pine trees overhead rustled. From far off came the sound of a hoot owl, and the outraged cry of some small animal caught in the claws of nature's plan.

Irving was getting in under the steering wheel. Reaching down Laurie Lee grabbed up a stone and sent it smashing through the windshield directly at Irving. The glass shattered, and Irving cursed.

As if hypnotized she watched without moving as Anthony rushed forward. Seeing what Laurie Lee had done, his face became consumed with rage.

"I'd rather be dead than see Andrew leave with you," she yelled.

Irving waited by Anthony's car as if uncertain what to do.

Laurie Lee had seen her now, and they seemed to have one thought as they circled Anthony. Elaine reached down and picked up a rock and hurled it at the car's radiator.

Laurie Lee reached for another rock, watching Anthony.

"Put that down," Anthony hollered, starting toward her. The light of his fluorescent lantern was tipped to cast the beam in her direction, blinding her.

"You're not taking Andrew," she screeched, her face contorted and white as Anthony waved at Irving and shouted, "Go. Go."

Irving started the motor. He drove slowly and carefully through weeds that hit against the car.

Elaine braced herself to face the verbal abuse that she knew would be forthcoming from an angry Anthony. But he wasn't even looking at her. He had turned to face Laurie Lee who had climbed on top of the rock wall, ready to run down the other side to cut off Irving when he reached the turn in the road. She was waving her arms as he drove past a thicket of trees and around the bend.

Laurie Lee balanced on the rocks, her arms still up, and watched as Irving drove off into the night.

Time stood still. For one heart-stopping moment Laurie Lee poised there, ready to rush forward. She seemed to sway, to waver in her purpose and as Elaine watched, she bent forward and then back as if she were participating in some ghastly dance. Then, all at once, before all of those who were keeping their eyes on her could make a move, she seemed to teeter, then buckle, as if she had no strength. She screamed once, then vanished from sight.

This time her scream was not of anger but of terror, of despair, of yielding to destiny.

Her cries echoed from the dark depths of the well into the starlit night, carrying across the distant hills, and into the wind that stirred the pine trees.

Then silence.

Normal night sounds became hushed as if the twittering birds and the restless animals of the Ozark forest waited, too, for the horrifying sound to be repeated.

But it never did.

Chapter Twenty-two

Shaking uncontrollably, Elaine sank to the ground on her knees, not fully understanding what happened. Anthony, the lantern in his hand, was bending over the rock wall, looking down. Disbelief was written on his face.

He straightened, and in the near dawn stared at Elaine.

"That's the old well that she told me about. She fell down. The same well . . ." His words were unintelligible. Mumbling. Incoherent. Gulping. Unable to continue.

"Get help," she told him, choking down a scream that kept rising again and again in her throat.

She'd never forget that scream of Laurie Lee's, so filled with despair, with resignation, and how it echoed so hopelessly across the hills.

"There's no use. She can't be alive."

"We must get her out. Get someone."

"The way she fell . . ." He shook his head. "I've got a phone in my car, but Irving has my car. She . . . Laurie Lee must have been driving hers. She used to keep one in her glove compartment. I'll go see if I can find where she left it."

Before he could make a move there was the sound of an engine, and they saw the rear lights of a car backing up and stop in the spot where Anthony's car had been parked, under the pine trees. The headlamps of another car came to a stop with the bumpers almost touching, blocking the road.

Irving got out. Anthony, without leaving the side of the well, motioned for him to come over. Mitchell got out of the other car and joined them, going over to Elaine.

"What's the matter? What's happened?" Mitchell held on to her as she almost collapsed.

"It's Laurie Lee," she choked, leaning against him, crying. "Anthony forced me and the kids to come here. Laurie Lee came looking for us, and Anthony shoved her down the well."

"What?" Anthony, startled, spun around to look at her.

"You heard me." Her chin came up.

Anthony was jerked forward by Irving's huge hand.

"What did you do to my sister?" he demanded, his voice rough and belligerent.

"Elaine's lying. I never touched her."

Irving let him go to lean over the well, peering down into the shaft, his shoulders heaving. Mitchell went over to him, warily putting one hand on Irving's shoulder.

"I can't see down. She can't have survived. It's a very deep well." Irving's voice broke. He straightened, his fists clenched. "If you did this, Anthony . . ."

"Why not ask what *she* did . . . killed your father, and Emma." Anthony scowled, and backed away.

"Laurie Lee killed my mother?" Mitchell's voice wasn't quite steady. "Why would she have done that?"

"Laurie Lee didn't deny it," Elaine said softly.

"Emma was working with me to get Aaron back," Anthony told him callously. "And Laurie Lee killed her."

"Working with . . . ? I can't believe it. You probably pushed Laurie Lee down yourself so you could blame her for my mother's death. Didn't you say, Elaine, that he did?"

"That's my story," she said, determined. "Unless . . ."

"Unless, what, Elaine? Unless what?" Anthony persisted, ignoring Irving's threatening attitude.

"I guess my story is up to you, Anthony. You brought me here, with the children, against my will. Kidnapping and murder. Even people like you can't get away from paying your dues forever."

Anthony rubbed his chin, his face haggard, his eyes cold and hard.

"Oh, hell," he said, and turned abruptly away. "Why should I bother? Get the boy out of my car," he told Mitchell, "and move yours out of the road."

Irving waited until Anthony had got in his car and driven away before sadly contemplating the situation. "It's like she was meant to end up this way. Like this was the end of something that started long ago. Do you believe in destiny?" he asked Elaine.

"She fell. It was an accident."

"I've got a phone on the front seat of my car, Irving," Mitchell said. "Call for help to get her out. I'll wait here with Elaine."

Elaine and Mitchell stood by the well, waiting with Irving until the authorities arrived. Only when Laurie Lee's broken body had been recovered from its watery grave, did they begin the long trip back to the pheasant farm with the children asleep in the back, while Irving returned in Laurie Lee's car.

"I find this all so hard to believe," Mitchell said over and over on the way home. She'd finished telling him, reluctantly, what Laurie Lee had said about Emma.

"I always said Mother would do anything that would benefit Laurie Lee, but even I didn't know how far she would go."

Later, when the children were in bed watched over by a subdued Pauline, they couldn't get the night's events out of their mind.

"To know Mother consorted with Anthony, thinking she was protecting Laurie Lee . . ." Mitchell couldn't let it go.

"I know," she said sympathetically. She held his hand.

"Irving tells me that one night their father tried to kill both of them by throwing them down that well. He yelled and kicked and got away and hid. His father knocked Laurie Lee down, but she grabbed hold of a rope. Thinking she fell, he went looking for Irving. While looking all over for *him,* Irving helped her out. Their father saw them and came at them again. Laurie Lee hit him with a rock, then she pushed him down the well. Then, Irving said they ran off into the timber and caught rides on the backs of trucks that were heading north. They never told authorities who they were or where they were from."

Elaine shuddered thinking of the childhood they must have had.

A week later, after Laurie Lee's funeral, Elaine and Mitchell walked with the children out by the pheasant pens.

"When Anthony signed the custody papers today," she said, "he told me that Laurie Lee was always afraid she'd be charged with murder if she admitted what she did. Later, she realized she wouldn't have, but by then she just wanted to avoid the publicity." Elaine sighed. "I don't think Anthony wanted Aaron or to get back at me anyway. He just wanted to exert his power to get even with Laurie Lee."

"Like he would have with you, if you hadn't turned his own way of doing things against him."

"He's agreed to the divorce. I told him I don't want alimony, and I don't want child support. I don't want the children raised on that kind of money. I'll get a job somewhere . . . doing something."

He pulled her aside, "I want to get to know you." he said softly.

"But you do?" she wondered.

He sighed and leaned his head against hers. "I don't know the real you. But I do know that wherever I am, I want you with me. Am I asking too much of you?"

"You could never ask too much," she said in a voice that wasn't quite steady.

Chapter Twenty-three

During the month following the tragedy Elaine had gone about like a robot, doing what needed to be done, helping Pauline in the kitchen, and trying to answer the children's endless questions without saying what she felt they were too young to hear.

One had to grieve. Working through it had been like being in a dark tunnel. She knew things would get brighter if she could keep on walking, day by day, one foot in front of the other until eventually she reached the end. Not "The End," but the other opening just ahead where the light shone, and life could begin anew.

So it was that she and Mitchell lived each day.

They weren't the only ones who were trying to overcome. On one of her daily walks to the pheasant pens with the children, she found Mitchell leaning on the board gate talking to Irving.

"I never dreamed Laurie Lee would . . ." Irving couldn't say the words. His voice broke.

The three of them stood in companionable silence.

"Nor I," Elaine finally said.

"I blame myself," Irving went on. "I can't change what

I did. I wish I could. Maybe if I hadn't conspired with Anthony she would still . . ."

"Don't think about the 'if's,' " Elaine told him. "We all could find use for that word. If I hadn't called Emma for help when I left Anthony . . ." She waved a helpless hand in the air.

"Anthony assured me that no one would get hurt, that he would act within the law."

"His law," Elaine pointed out. "Money was his law. And relying on his lawyer who is no better than Anthony."

"She would have hated what the media would have published about her," Irving said grimly.

Mitchell placed a comforting hand on Irving's shoulder. "Do you know yet what you're going to do with the business?"

Elaine was reminded that Laurie Lee's will stated: *To my loving relative, Irving, I leave . . .*

Irving's smile was lopsided with the irony of him inheriting the cosmetic business.

"You can't make eagle feathers out of a pheasant's tail," he said. "What would Veronica and I do with the cosmetic business? We've decided to sell our interests, and I might add that that decision is a great relief to everyone concerned."

Mitchell nodded his head in approval.

"What are you going to do?" Irving glanced first at Elaine and then at Mitchell.

"Taking care of my children is my primary concern," Elaine said without hesitation. All of them turned to look at Aaron and Amanda who were standing outside the wire fence watching the pheasants. They made a pleasing picture.

Amanda, who had become more courageous over time, had a chubby hand poked through the wire, offering a fistful of corn. Aaron gently pulled her hand back, and demonstrated how she should toss it through the fence into the birds.

"Well, Veronica and I plan to go to Florida. I promised her before we were ever married that we'd go, and I've never heard the end of it since." Irving didn't appear too thrilled at the prospect. "That's why I agreed to help Anthony."

"I can't decide if I should accept what Laurie Lee left to me." Mitchell sounded weary and drew one hand across his eyes. "Doesn't seem right somehow."

Elaine quoted the lawyer's words as he read the will: "To Mitchell Madison, the son of my dearest friend, Emma Madison, and in accordance with her wishes, all that I intended leaving to her, I leave to him as follows . . ."

"That's what she wanted," Elaine stated. "And what your mother wanted."

They stood close together and watched Irving walk toward the feed shed where Russ was working. Russ had never slacked off after Laurie Lee's death. Like Pauline, who put the same good food on the table like she'd always done, Russ continued to give full measure for his wages and would until the end of the month. Then, he and Pauline were taking the inheritance that Laurie Lee left to them, and moving to California.

But until he was ready to leave Russ would keep everything going outside just as Pauline would do inside. Mitchell confided to Elaine that he hadn't been much help. Couldn't keep his mind on his work, he said.

"What do you intend to do?" Elaine persisted.

"With what Laurie Lee left me?" He shook his head and put an arm around her waist, pulling her close. "I don't know. I just know I want us to be together."

"Do you still want to go west . . . or north and have a farm where you can raise cattle?"

"If you're with me. You haven't said what you'd like to do."

She wasn't surprised at his words. There had always been an attraction between them. "I want to be with you," she admitted. "And I think I might get so I like cattle."

His arms held her tighter. "It'll be a gamble, you know."

"What isn't?"

She smiled up at him, and nodded toward the children who were busily playing and paying them no attention. "I come with a lot of baggage," she warned.

His eyes held a wary faraway look. "So do I," he confided. "And mine may be more troublesome than yours."

She realized he still grieved, not only over his mother's death, but knowing about the wrong Emma did by conspiring with Anthony. That knowledge cut deep, almost as deep as her death.

"I'm glad Laurie Lee put the farm in trust for Aaron until he's twenty-one. At least by then he can be told that he had a mother who really cared for him."

Laurie Lee had plainly stated, "To Andrew, my son, I do hereby . . ."

"Do you suppose she had a foreboding of what was to come?" Mitchell interrupted her thoughts.

"I don't believe that."

He smiled. "I guess I don't either, but I have heard . . ."

"If I want to hear that stuff I'll go talk to Pauline," she teased, then sobered thoughtfully. "The children are certainly too young to take all this in. Sometimes this past month I've even wondered if I'm too young." She wrinkled her nose ruefully.

"They needn't know everything," Mitchell had said. "Let them keep their innocence."

Elaine agreed. Laurie Lee was beyond punishment here on earth, and Emma was guilty only of an all too human frailty: a misguided sense of duty causing her to betray those who loved and trusted her.

Thinking of the future when Aaron must face the fact that Laurie Lee was his real mother, they only told him that

Laurie Lee accidently lost her life while trying to stop his father from leaving with him.

Aaron came running up. Amanda followed close behind. In one hand Aaron held a long green feather which he had retrieved from the pheasant pen. He held it up for her to admire.

"I've been thinking, Laine." His dark eyes were squinting in the sun and from his concentration on the feather he twirled between his fingers. "I think Laurie Lee really was Green Feather, don't you?"

Elaine couldn't answer. Someday she'd tell him the truth about who Laurie Lee really was. But not yet.

He needed to feel that life could be less complicated, more reliable, less fearful, and that beyond a shadow of a doubt, he needed the assurance that people loved him. He needed to know that his place in her heart was permanent.

They started toward the yard, Aaron's free hand in hers while the other twirled the green feather. Mitchell swung Amanda up to ride on his shoulders. They went through the gate and up the walk. He stood Amanda down and she and Aaron raced across the yard toward the back part of the house.

"Whatever we decide to do, we'll decide together," he said, smiling tenderly.

Together. Together they would make whatever plans were needed to take them into the future.

He put his arms around her. "We're both in the same boat, you and I. Both at loose ends."

"In the same boat?" she tipped her head back to look up at him teasingly, "Are we sailing then?"

"You mean you can't feel the waves?" He gave her a long and passionate kiss.

"Um-m-m, yes. Yes, now I can."

"Good." He stared deep into her eyes for a moment before drawing her even closer. "Then just don't rock the boat."